ANGELKILLER

ANGELKILLER

H. DAVID BLALOCK

SEVENTH STAR PRESS

Cover art and illustrations: Matthew Perry
Cover art and illustrations in this book copyright © 2011 Matthew Perry
& Seventh Star Press, LLC.

Editor: Amanda DeBord

Published by Seventh Star Press, LLC.

ISBN Number 9780983740230

Library of Congress Control Number: 2011941721

Seventh Star Press
www.seventhstarpress.com
info@seventhstarpress.com

Publisher's Note:
Angelkiller is a work of fiction. All names, characters, and places are
the product of the author's imagination, used in fictitious manner.
Any resemblances to actual persons, places, locales, events, etc.
are purely coincidental.

Printed in the United States of America

First Edition

DEDICATION

To my family, and especially the one
who inspires me on a daily basis,
Maria

1

Chandler sat in the virtual interaction seat, the computer screen's multicolored lights flickering over his face. The I/O set hung loosely from one ear, the other side of the set caught between his lolling head and his right shoulder. The chair slowly rotated as his body's center of gravity shifted, creaking slightly, until the I/O set clattered to the floor as Chandler's body crumpled limply off its perch onto the hardwood floor.

The other person in the room unscrewed the silencer from the end of the weapon and tucked both items into the deep pockets of his dark uniform jacket. He pulled artificial skin covering over his own hands and straightened the chair, gazing at Chandler's body for a moment before sinking into the chair himself. Within a matter of seconds, he accessed the security settings relative to Chandler's personal account. Slipping a small portable device from another pocket, he plugged it into the CPU and began the process of changing the parameters.

Ten minutes later, he reached over to turn off the computer. He pulled the CPU free of its peripheral cables and, with one last look around, carried it out of the apartment.

Beside Chandler's unmoving form, a metallic cylinder stood gently ticking. A few seconds after the stranger left, the ticking stopped. Chandler couldn't hear the soft hissing of the gas, not that it would have made any difference to him. Nor would the tiny click of the sparking device left behind by his visitor have alarmed him.

Death comes but once to all men.

2

Centuries.

To most people, that was just a word; an abstract, practically incomprehensible measurement of time. It was a word used to convey a sense of timelessness because of the inability of the average person to grasp its true nature, a nature that spanned whole lifetimes, even those of entire nations or civilizations. Trying to understand the truth of centuries was like trying to picture the length of a river in one's head. It reached a point beyond which one disconnects from the real and launches into the unreal, from physical understanding into mental imagination.

To remember a lifetime of events, of joy and sorrow, success and failure, was hard enough. To remember centuries of a lifetime would be too much for one mind to endure. Eventually the things of the past would become entwined with the present. Events of today would inevitably remind one of something long gone by. Nature is, after all, a series of cycles: seasons without end, life and death and life again. Nothing ever truly ends, because for there to be an end means there must have been a beginning, and if one lived too long that beginning becomes meaningless.

Jonah Mason puffed on the Montecristo cigar as he slowly rode his glider rocker on the porch and gazed into the pale blue sky above the trees that shielded his house from the country road that ran quiet and gray to the south. He listened to the murmur of crickets in the early evening air and watched the lengthening shadows across the close-cropped grass that stretched out the sixty feet to those sentinel boles. At the end of the white gravel drive that pierced the trees' defenses he could just see the open iron gates flanked by token brick wings that separated them from the mailbox standing silent vigil across the road.

The name on the mailbox was, and was not, his. It was an expedience, an allowance to the times, another in an endless series of pseudonyms that hid who he really was from a world that could never envisage the truth. Here at his retreat, he could ignore the demands of the twenty-second century world outside. The soft hum of a small, invisible aircraft somewhere overhead reminded him briefly of his days in France early in the twentieth century. He pushed away the bloody visions that precipitated. The faint tapping of a woodpecker at work in the trees brought memories of times much further back, when airplanes were unknown and country roads were little more than dirt tracks carved from virgin forests. An automobile passed by, its tires sounding like a shadow of the rushing waters that swept away an army long ago in the plains of Achaia, an event only he, of all mankind, now remembered. Lost to history like a million other moments, unremembered, forgotten by all but himself.

He was the seventh son of a seventh son. His father was Sextus Vernus, and he became Septimus Vernus. Although they were simple farmers, it was an auspicious birth, said the oracle, and one that would bring great honor to his family.

If he survived, he thought grimly.

The words of the oracle haunted him as he had fought like the lion whose image adorned his shield, piling enemy bodies around him in a carnal landscape of hacked and bleeding corpses. His gladius, bent and nicked, finally was ripped from his hands by a heavy blow and he resorted to bashing his opponents with the shield, using the spike in its center as he would a spear.

They were raiders, but they were fierce and expert

fighters. He suspected they had come up from the south, sailing from Utica to harass the Campani coastline, hoping to drive into Rome. They might be the vanguard of another force sent against Scipio, or they might just be pirates taking advantage of the conflict with Carthage. Whoever they were, he did not intend to allow them to enter Liternum without a fight.

Rome had been at war with Carthage all his life. It was simply a fact of everyday existence, and one that gave his own life purpose and goal. He lived to serve Rome, to bend his arm and heart to her service. He had marched with his company along the Popilian Way from the Falernian District to Picentia and back a hundred times, patrolling and watching for just such an incursion.

And finally it had come. Now all the years of training were put to the test, and Vernus dove into the fighting with gusto, willing to die to protect his beloved Rome.

Time stood still as they came at him again and again, draped in their strange garb and wielding swords, pikes, and spears to take his life. Reduced to his shield and bare hands, he knew it was just a matter of time, as did the enemy, but he would not go easily. Grimly, he held on, pushing them back, bashing at them again and again. The lion-shield threw aside sword strikes, brushed away spear thrusts, and stunted off pikes driven at him.

There was a pause in the attacks and he found himself the only man of his company still standing. The enemy soldiers pulled back in their circle around him and held a tight perimeter, their weapons readied at him but not advancing. Confused, he slowly spun around, ready at a second's notice to defend himself, but the enemy seemed content to wait.

A man in an ornate breastplate stepped forward through the perimeter to face him. The man was obviously an officer, but the words he barked at Vernus made no sense. Suddenly, an older man, in priestly robes recognizable only because Vernus had seen pilgrims to Rome in similar garb, pushed his way through to stand beside the officer and held up a hand for silence. The officer reluctantly bowed and stepped back to allow the holy man forward.

"Valiant man," the priest said in halting Latin, "I salute you."

Vernus eyed him with suspicion and kept his peace. The priest held his hands out wide to show he was unarmed, but that did nothing to ease Vernus' mind.

"Know you, valiant man, that Hannibal is coming this way and will soon leave Italy for his home."

A cold chill went through Vernus. He had heard of the

Carthaginian general, but the idea he might be this far south was frightening. Had Rome fallen? Was he fighting for nothing?

"What is your name?" the priest asked amiably.

Vernus held his peace, warily eyeing the others.

"I am Sorius," the other went on. "I am Celtiberian, but I serve only God. Do you understand me?"

Vernus had no idea what a Celtiberian was. He thought it might be some kind of wizard, considering the way the enemy fighters treated the man with such obvious respect. As to which God the man referred to, did it matter? He sensed the beginnings of a possibility he might actually survive this battle. Hesitantly, Vernus nodded, still holding himself ready for the attack he feared might come soon.

Sorius turned to the officer and said something in the unknown language that greatly irritated the man. There was a brief, heated exchange, then, with one last dark look at Vernus, the officer signaled the men surrounding his Roman foe to move back. Vernus watched in amazement as they formed up and moved off toward the coast, leaving them alone. Sorius waited until the others were out of sight around a bend in the road before speaking again.

"Now, let us reason together," he said.

Vernus frowned.

"You must understand," Sorius began, "it was never our intention to attack your villages here. We are traveling to my home in Gaul. It was your commander who ordered the attack. We were defending ourselves." He smiled and held his hands outstretched. "I am an old man of some influence, and so my lord requires I have an escort whenever I travel. I deeply regret this has happened, but once it began there was little I could do to stop it. Please believe me when I say, I have no ill will toward you or your people."

Vernus was not sure exactly what the man was planning, but there was something about him that felt right, as if, now that he had the time to consider it, he recognized the man and knew he could be trusted. It didn't occur to him to question this sudden feeling of security. He simply accepted it and lowered his shield.

The holy man smiled. "Thank you. Please, would you accompany me for a while? At least until I rejoin my guard?"

The request seemed reasonable, given the old man's obvious fragility. Vernus searched for his weapon among the dead and tucked the gladius into its scabbard. He motioned the holy man to proceed and fell into step beside him.

* * *

Sorius proved to be a true academic, drenched in the knowledge of centuries, knowledge both mundane and divine. He unreservedly shared this with Vernus as they walked, and the younger man found himself joining the troop in their northward trek as if he had always been with them. Despite Sorius' outward physical appearance, Vernus could sense an inner power whose presence grew daily. There was much more to this man than met the eye. The depth of his understanding of humanity and its history was astounding. When he spoke of events long past, events spanning continents and centuries, Vernus got the idea he was not just speaking abstractly, but from personal experience. His curiosity about the man prompted him to fall into step with the bodyguard when they overtook the small company. After a few annoyed glances, the others accepted him grudgingly.

The remainder of their march proceeded uneventfully. Even as they approached the vicinity of Rome herself, they were seldom challenged and never resisted. Vernus was at first disturbed at this apparent lack of concern over the security of his beloved Rome, but he was soon distracted by his fascination with Sorius.

The holy man did indeed live in a large compound near the coast of southern Gaul. Vernus learned that a Celtiberian, far from being a wizard, was simply the name of a native of this area. Sorius' family had worked the land around his home for years, and his influence with the local chieftains afforded him a certain amount of immunity to attack from the raiding parties that frequently hit the coastal villages. He was a figure of almost legendary awe to the tribes and actually did have a reputation as a magician for his healing abilities and tactical sense. Vernus recognized the man's military bent early on in their relationship and sensed that Sorius had not always been a pilgrim. His aptitude with the sword and spear belied his clerical lifestyle.

Sorius took Vernus under his wing. He taught his new acolyte to read and write, and educated him in the philosophies of men and gods, transforming him from the backwoods farmer cum soldier he was into what would many years later be referred to as a "renaissance man." Within Sorius' sanctum, Vernus came to know himself and the world around him ever more deeply. Months passed as his education continued unabated until finally, one day, Sorius brought him into the sanctum to tell him something Vernus had previously suspected but never thought true.

"My time grows short, Vernus, my son," Soris said as he shuffled through the mountain of papers that filled the three tables and shelves in the sanctum. Dozens of candles lit the room, the hissing of their wax a constant background to the whisper of vellum against wood. "In just a few years, I will be recalled to my Master. I am ready, but I need to be sure you will be ready."

"I do not understand, my lord," Vernus said. "Recalled? Are you going away?"

Sorius smiled at him over the manuscript he put on the table. "You need not be concerned about me. Let us concentrate on you." He opened the manuscript and motioned Vernus to stand beside him. "You must learn what I know, if you are to be my heir."

Vernus was stunned. "Your heir?"

"Yes, my son, you are to take my place. Had you not guessed?" Sorius laughed at Vernus' expression. "I see you suspected. Good. Then you have already begun to accept." He indicated the manuscript. "I have written within this book everything I believe you need to understand what has gone before. You will need this in the future, when you doubt, and you will doubt. I will tell you what is in this book, but you must promise me you will protect it until such time as your doubts are gone. Swear this to me."

"I so swear."

"Good. Now, let us begin."

What Sorius told him then boggled his mind so badly it took days to understand fully. For a man of his time, Vernus had never even considered the possibility of the events Sorius outlined. Nor would he come to understand them for years.

At the beginning of time, Sorius said, there had been a great War. Forces far beyond man had battled over dominion of the Earth. In the end, the darker forces had gained the upper hand over those of the Light. They had taken residence on Earth, building great cities and civilizations, convincing men that *they* were the true Masters, the givers of all things beneficial. They educated men in the arts of war and death and destruction. The forces of Light had never abandoned the Conflict, but it became harder and harder to convince those few they contacted on Earth of the Truth. Men's minds became more and more like their Masters' and turned away from the Light with increasing frequency.

But the forces of Light began building as well, behind the scenes, out of sight of the majority of men. An Army of Light formed, based on knowledge of the Truth, dedicated to bringing that Light to the world and deposing the destructive spirit that crippled the growth of humankind. Sorius was only the latest in a long line of leaders of that Army, and he had lived for centuries, guiding it, building it, growing it, and directing it. So far, they had served as little more than informants to the forces of Light, spies in the great Conflict. Sorius' vision was that someday The Army would help in more concrete ways, replacing the allies of The Enemy with those of the Light, installing men of good heart and vision in places of authority and bringing mankind out of the dark.

Such a vision took time to achieve, and Sorius, long-lived as he might be, was still mortal. His time was fast approaching, and he had chosen Vernus to take up the mantle after him. It was an awesome, daunting responsibility, but from the time Sorius saw him fight there on the coast of Italy, the holy man knew Vernus had the quality of spirit that could accomplish the necessary.

Vernus asked no questions as Sorius spoke, too overwhelmed by the sheer scope of what Sorius related to form coherent thought. It never occurred to him to doubt what Sorius said. The truth of it rang in his spirit and sang in his mind. Somewhere deep inside him, he had known this all along. Only now, with it flatly and plainly stated, did he understand.

Over the next few years, Sorius and Vernus were inseparable. The younger man soaked up the elder's knowledge, finally finding his voice to ask questions and slowly coming to grips with the truth. Nearly a decade passed before he discovered the secret of Sorius' long life.

He had been exercising in the compound's green, where the holy man's guard had erected a practice field. Standing pells, scarred and splintered by innumerable sword strikes, were arrayed on one side of the field while sand pits scored by heavy use and stained with spilled blood covered the other. At the far end of the field and against the compound's thick wall were seven targets used for both archery and javelin practice. Seldom was the field completely empty, and that day Vernus was wielding his gladius against another of the guard in the sand pits. The men went after each other with alacrity, sparing no effort, for they had to be able to test their own and their compatriot's skill to its uttermost.

"Vernus!" he heard someone shout.

The distraction, should it have been anyone else, would never have fazed him. He was used to the screams and shouts of the enemy and wounded on the battlefield. However, there was something about this voice that rang in his ears oddly and he staggered, stunned, just as his opponent's weapon swung for him. He was barely able to take the major brunt of the blow on his shield, but the blade still bit deeply into his side. Bright pain washed over him as he dropped to his knees. He heard shouting from far off and guessed it was the guard coming to his aid, but the darkness that closed over him shut out both light and sound.

He was floating on a gentle sea, a breeze filling the boat's sail and pushing the little vessel along. He couldn't see land anywhere around him, but that didn't alarm him as much as the brilliant figure that stood at the bow. He couldn't quite make out a face, but the body of the figure was vaguely humanoid, with two arms, two legs, a torso and a head. It was difficult to look directly at it without squinting in pain. He knew he should be afraid, or at least alarmed, but he couldn't find it in himself to be either.

"Where am I?" he asked.

The other didn't answer, but pointed with one of its arms off to his left. He looked that way and was surprised to see a shoreline close by that he had not seen moments before. On the shore he could clearly see Sorius watching him.

"Master?" he asked. He raised his voice to carry to the shore. "Master!"

"Have no fear, my son," Sorius' voice came clear in his head in spite of the distance between them. "Trust me."

The boat pulled away from the shoreline. He watched until Sorius was too small to make out anymore before turning back to his shipmate. He wanted to ask it where they were going, but there seemed little purpose in that. The other had no mouth to respond.

"You are chosen," a voice told him.

He looked around, but there was nothing different. It finally hit him that the figure at the bow was communicating with him without physical speech.

"Chosen?" Vernus answered.

"For another life."

Now fear set in. Tales of Charon and the river Styx thundered in his mind. Wasn't he supposed to give the ferryman a coin for this trip? And didn't Hades lie on the other side?

"You see what you expect to see," the voice went on in his head. "Not the reality."

The statement confused him, but he felt comforted at its tone. "What do you mean by another life?"

There was a moment's pause before the response came.

"You are now a Soldier in a Conflict greater than any you can imagine."

The crunch of gravel under wheels brought Mason back to the present. He watched impassively as the black sedan slowly crept through the iron gates and rolled down the drive toward him. Its windows, tinted black and opaque in the distance, hid its occupants but he had an idea who it might be.

He flicked the half-smoked cigar into the yard and glowered at the intruder. The sedan rolled to a stop beside the house. He didn't leave his seat. If they wanted to speak to him, they would have to come out of their anonymous shelter and face him.

The front passenger door opened and a large man dressed in a suit as black and nondescript as the car rose from inside to glance around suspiciously from behind dark glasses. Mason watched him slowly make his way to the back of the sedan and open the rear passenger door. An even larger man appeared now, standing and stretching as if wakening from sleep. This man turned toward Mason and, with a deliberate step, approached, followed closely by the other.

Mason could feel the power flowing off the man even before he was close enough to smell the telltale odor so similar to lilac, yet a subtlety of that fragrance that could not be duplicated by any means known to man. That scent emanated from only one type of being: a Minion of The Enemy. And usually only when they were contemplating mischief.

"Mister Jonah Mason?" the larger man asked when he was about five steps away.

Mason waited. The man took his silence as a positive

response.

"My name is Dorian Azrael. May I have a word?"

He let the man stand there for a moment while he digested the name. Dorian Azrael. Appropriate enough, he supposed. He sighed. It had to happen eventually. His extended time away from direct confrontation with The Enemy had at last come to an end. He was just surprised it had taken this long. Best to get this over with quickly, as he could feel the familiar dryness in the back of his throat brought on by that psychic drain all Minions exuded. His personal wards protected him from the brunt of that influence, but the sourness of that vacuum where a soul should be made him uncomfortable.

Rising from his glider rocker, Mason went inside, leaving the door open. Although Azrael could come in, it certainly wasn't the invitation he knew the man wanted. It was best to keep some permissions in abeyance until he knew more. The other man, probably no more than a bodyguard, remained outside.

The front room was heavily warded, and they both knew it. What Azrael probably didn't know was that the wards were based on ancient writings Sorius said came from a library destroyed by a flood long before he was born. He had called them Nephil wards and attributed their effectiveness to

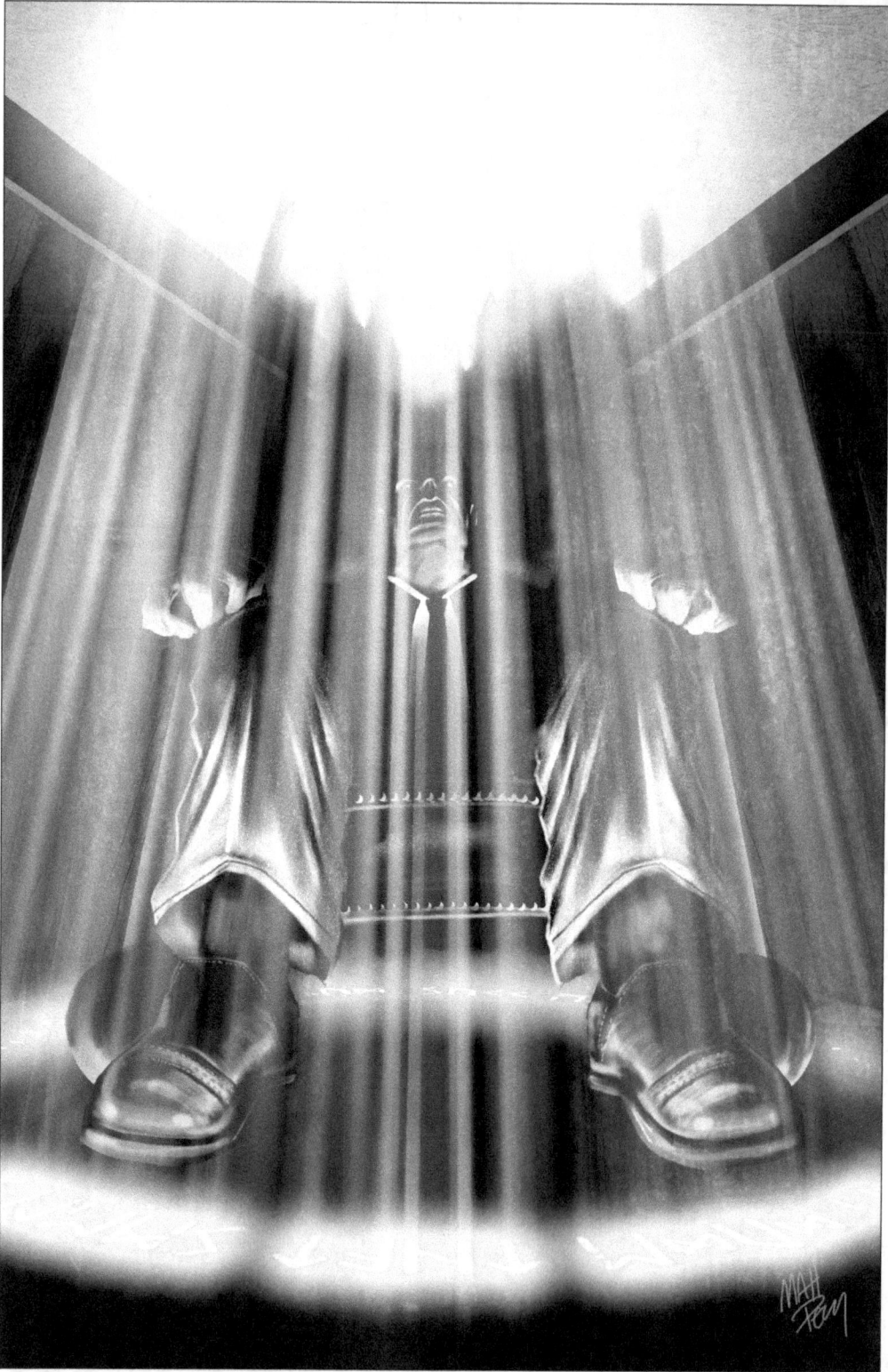

the skill of an ancient magician named Laban. That magician taught men about the esoteric arts, claiming to have been given the knowledge by a being named Tiphereth. When Mason learned the angelic script and found that name in several of Sorius' older tomes, he understood just how powerful any ward invoking that name could be, for the Dark or the Light. Sorius had been very careful to impress on him that the usage of any ward was not a guarantee of protection, no matter how powerful it might be. The fact that Azrael stepped across the threshold with difficulty but made no complaint demonstrated the truth of that warning. The wards kept minor entities at bay very effectively. That Azrael had penetrated the wards testified to his power, but the pain involved in breaking those wards had to have been excruciating. That told Mason much. It meant things had progressed to the point that negotiations were being sought by both sides regardless of personal consequences. Not a good sign.

The wards re-sealed after Azrael's entrance, like a vault door closing. Inside the warded room, Azrael had to know he was abdicating a large portion of his ability to affect Mason. He was cut off from the source of his power, or at least crippled.

Mason sat in one of the two high-backed chairs that dominated the room, the one that faced the door. Except for a small, bare table, no other furniture graced the room and the walls were free of visible ornamentation. Azrael took the opposite chair unbidden and sighed as he sank into it.

"I understand your distrust," Azrael began, "but as you see, I have come unarmed and unescorted."

Mason sincerely doubted that assertion, but he crossed his legs and placed his hands on the chair's padded arms. Best let the other speak until his point was made before responding. Long, hard experience had taught him that lesson. His silence seemed to annoy the other, who scowled and leaned forward.

"Very well, straight to the heart of the matter," Azrael said. "We know who you really are and I have come to warn you off."

Keeping his expression impassive, Mason eyed Azrael. He had suspected The Enemy knew his real identity. That was really not much of a surprise. How they had found out was of no real importance at the moment. What mattered was their intent.

"Warn me off what?" he asked, neutrally.

"Come now, don't insult me with such a question," Azrael replied. "We know you have been recruited and assigned."

As he watched Azrael speak, the scent of lilac grew

stronger. He saw the beginnings of the attack in the brightening of the wards around him and was frankly surprised. The man was in a warded room. Surely he must be aware of the danger, the risk he was running. Was he so sure of his own abilities as to ignore that? Or was he so contemptuous of Mason's?

"The end of this Conflict is at hand, Vernus," Azrael growled, "and..."

The pronunciation of his name set off the first ward. The front door slammed shut and the room instantly sealed. Azrael had the presence of mind not to suddenly move, sparing himself the brunt of the attack. The circle flared around the chair he occupied and the air crackled with the scent of roses. Light flared across Azrael's frame, a burst of pure power that surrounded him and burned brightly for several seconds.

"No names," Mason told him, calmly.

Azrael leaned back in the chair, frowning. He would need a moment to gather his thoughts, Mason surmised. He knew the strength and speed of the wards must have been a surprise to Azrael. No doubt the man was accustomed to easier prey. Over time he must have become overconfident. The greatest advantage Mason knew he had was the fact he was still outwardly human, even to the sensibilities of those like Azrael. They were conditioned to expect certain reactions, certain abilities in their human foe. If the opponent showed capabilities outside or beyond those expectations, they became confused. Unable to adapt to the novelty, they usually retreated or pressed forward harder, depending on the urgency of their mission. It was ironic that the very thing that made them what they were, the thing they could not deny, was what they hated most: single-minded purpose. The mission was paramount. Their own survival was secondary. Oh, they could retreat to regroup and rethink their strategy, but they always returned. The Enemy never, ever, abandoned a mission once assigned. It was simply impossible.

"Warn me off what?" he asked again.

The visitor cleared his throat and smiled weakly. "It seems I have been hasty and taken undue liberties," he said. "My apologies."

Mason nodded his acknowledgment. Azrael hesitated a moment, as if he expected the wards to be removed, but Mason knew better. Obviously, Azrael had a low estimate of his intelligence. Well, the man would simply have to be continually surprised.

"So," Azrael continued finally, "in answer to your question, we *advise* you not to interfere with our plans for the next few months."

"I see," Mason answered. "And why would I?"

"We merely wish to avoid any form of confrontation. We thought it best to clarify our position with you now rather than fall into an unfortunate misunderstanding later."

"Misunderstanding?"

Azrael's smile broadened as he recovered his aplomb. "We intend to take some actions soon that have, in the past, been judged by some as, how shall I put this? — 'hostile' to some people. Please, do not misinterpret our actions. We only wish to set right those things that have gone out of balance. It is an unfortunate truth that people may be hurt, but let me again assure you that is never our intention." He paused and appeared to wait for Mason to respond. When the silence remained unbroken, he cleared his throat. "May we count on your cooperation?"

Mason stood slowly. Azrael, still acutely aware of the electric atmosphere, instinctively rose as well.

"I will take your warning under consideration," Mason said.

Azrael started to retort, then stopped himself and made a slight bow. "We thank you," he said. "I am certain we understand one another."

"We do."

Releasing the wards around his visitor, Mason escorted the man through the door. As the black sedan rolled back out toward the road, he lit another Montecristo and thought about the last time he had been 'warned off'. Had it been 300 years already?

He had traveled from the smoke-filled, terrified cities of war-torn Europe to the relative quiet of America, following the urgings of Central Command to establish an Army cell in the new country. He found a people still embracing the notions of Truth and charity, a welcome change from the despair and fatigue of a Europe worn down by centuries of pointless battles and suffering. However, even in the infant nation, nothing seemed to have changed for many people. Once more, he remembered the lesson.

The question "why do bad things happen to good people?" that plagued philosophers and clerics had a very simple answer. In the Great War between Good and Evil, Evil had come out the victor. The Truth about this was hidden from most of humanity because the victors wrote the history. In the minds of men, evil became the good and *vice versa*. There were, however, a few who knew the Truth, and that few, calling themselves The Army, waged a continuing war against The Enemy. It was, in the eyes of most, a silly superstitious exercise, a childish play wrought by ignorant people fascinated with conspiracy theories. Mason had heard the ridicule, had often listened to the rationalization of human leaders at the atrocities perpetrated by The Enemy. Mason heard the inherent paradox in those assertions, even if the purveyors of the explanations did not. It was his job to educate, to enlighten, and sometimes to engage in combat with the forces that supported the substructure maintaining the illusion that The Enemy were the rightful rulers of humanity.

He found a ready pool of recruits in the infant nation. He also found The Enemy already seeking to tear down what the people had so laboriously built. They knew of his arrival almost immediately. He was hard to miss, and his reputation preceded him, the name he had used for so many years too well known. A man met him at the hotel just after he checked in, someone who should not have known him, and addressed him by name.

It was not an auspicious beginning.

The telephone ringing woke him from his thoughts.

"Yes?"

"Meeting in fifteen. You know where."

"On my way."

* * *

The voice on the phone was Aorld Maachen, one of the other five agents in North America. German born, he had immigrated to America just before the First World War, changing his name to Harold Martin for expediency sake. Mason had personally recruited him during the Second World War.

Martin had procured employment in a large technology company whose main product was to become the vehicle for a battleground inconceivable to most even by the end of the twentieth century – computers. Specifically, virtual reality generators and programs.

While the rest of the world considered environments like the Internet and massive multi-player online games little more than idle entertainment, an entire substructure was developed. Incursions from this substructure, where a combat of powers unknown to the outside world was conceived and executed, manifested into the overlying networks in the forms of computer viruses. The baffled technicians who struggled with them called them 'malware.'

In spite of the obvious risks involved in the vulnerability of programming to these often seemingly spontaneous "bugs," companies continued to pursue increasingly more complex and personal devices. By the end of the 1990s, most households in the developed nations contained at least one computer connected to this global infrastructure. Individuals began to become dependent on them for basic economic and social interaction, and inevitably even guidance for personal decision making. Even governments interacted internally and externally through the system that floated on a subsystem whose depths went unnoticed except by those whose special knowledge gave them access.

Mason was one of those few.

Getting to the meeting place required he enter a massive multiplayer online game, or MMORPG. Access was simple, the same as for anyone who partook of its escape from the mundane life. However, the similarity of Mason's experience within the game stopped there. The interface equipment he used, although it was an older model, was light-years beyond anything available even to the most advanced research facilities in the outside world.

The product of over thirty years of design, improvement, and innovation, the Army interface combined a system of communication and exchange underneath the game's graphics and audio. The crude virtual reality of the game was a thin skin over the profound virtual reality of The Army's system. The chair

Mason used interacted with the nerves of his spine to provide a channel directly to his brain, while the I/O set he wore around his neck enabled him to speak through subcutaneous circuitry with others in the invisible world. The I/O also enabled him to track his physical body's vital signs, critical to his safety as it was easy to become so involved in the virtual reality as to forget himself there.

He logged on and slipped the I/O set around his neck. The computer webcam flickered briefly as the system's face recognition software read his visage. He leaned forward at the prompt to allow the cam to scan his retina, pulling away at the tone indicating the process was complete. He ignored the tickle as the I/O set sampled, analyzed, and transmitted the information about his DNA from his perspiration. Leaning back, he closed his eyes and turned inward, following brilliant flares of light behind his eyelids as the chair connected.

The agreed place used to be a town outside Oklahoma City, Oklahoma, strangely called Yukon. If there was a location less like that Alaskan wilderness, Mason didn't know of it. Springing from the flatlands like a lonely stand of trees in a desert, Yukon then was an oasis in the great Dust Bowl. Over the years, time was kind to the little burg, but the encroachment of the Oklahoma City suburbs drove them away from it as a safe meeting place.

There was a brief blackness, then he found himself in the familiar surroundings of E-Yukon. Martin had designed the place to replicate their old meeting site, a white clapboard farmhouse set off the main highway by a wheat field that waved under eternally amber skies. Although it resided within the confines of an online game, access to E-Yukon was only available to those Martin allowed.

He glanced around for a moment, taking in the bleakness of the area and marveling again at the faithfulness to its original. He felt the dryness of the hot wind, tasted the grit that floated on it. For all intents and purposes, he was back in Yukon and it was 1933, the world was on the brink of a catastrophic war that would kill tens of millions, change the balance of power from the Old World to the New, and signal the beginning of a Conflict that would be waged out of sight of the rest of humanity for centuries to come.

He had long ago stopped trying to differentiate between this reality and the one he had left behind. It simply wasn't worth the effort. Distractions of that kind merely hampered his ability to move and act in this world, a world that was becoming more and more critical to the world outside.

He climbed the creaking stairs to the wooden porch. A

bench swing hung from rusted chains to his right. Curled up on it, an old dog opened one rheumy eye and considered him long enough to determine it wasn't worth the effort to get down from his comfortable perch to challenge Mason's approach. The dog yawned, showing yellowed, rotting teeth, then settled back into his nap with a perfunctory growl.

The worn screen door whined as he opened it and slapped shut behind him with an annoyed bang. As he stood for a moment adjusting to the darkness inside, he heard voices coming from his right. He could make out Martin's clipped English, the drawl belonging to Stephen Overguard, the nasal New England bark sported by John Tripp, and the quiet murmur that could only be the newest member of their group, Janice Meeker. They proved to be seated around a table in the kitchen, its red and white plaid tablecloth worn through in places to show the dark wood. The smell of hot coffee and sweet pastries drew Mason to an empty seat beside Martin. Another empty seat stood beside Overguard.

"Where's Chandler?" he asked, sipping the coffee and reaching for a roll.

"Dead."

Martin's retort caught him by surprise. "Dead? What happened?"

"We're not sure. That's why we're here."

"Hmmm," he replied. The coffee was unusually good this time. Mason looked at Tripp. "Yours?" he asked, indicating the cup.

"Aye. Picked up the code in New Haven. How is it?"

Mason nodded his approval. "Better than Overguard's."

The offended agent scowled at him. "I don't see you ever trying," he said.

"Boys," Janice interrupted. "I think we have more important things to discuss."

Overguard laughed. "What's wrong, Jan? Afraid we'll hurt each other?"

"Words have power everywhere, Stephen. You know that."

"All right, all right," Martin put in. "Let me fill you in on what I know." The rest lapsed into silence as he went on. "About six hours ago, I got a ping from Chandler that the targets he was tracking were netting, but the encryption was new. I immediately booted and jumped the net to his coords, but there was a block just over his central. At first, I thought he was walled against intrusion while he worked on the decryption, but none of the passwords he'd given me worked. After about ten minutes the block cleared. Chandler was down. And out."

A few moments passed while they considered the information. None of them had to ask who "the targets" were, but the idea of an agent walled so completely was stunning. The latest protocols were less than 36 hours old, designed by Central and randomized on site. The security was far better than anything available anywhere else, making the best mundane governmental protocols look like substitution code in comparison. There were only a few possibilities presented that would enable The Enemy to crack that security, none of which bode well.

"Nothing in his stores to indicate details about what he'd found?" Overguard asked.

"He was wiped," Martin said grimly. "Zeroed."

That hit them hard. Agent archives were connected to Central through a massive encoding, different from the site security, but to wipe the archive meant someone had bypassed not only the entry codes, but the memory stamps as well. It was not likely the intruder could have reverse-tracked to Central, but if they could access one agent, it meant a major breach. Chandler's contacts would have to be immediately isolated and de-linked.

"Any fingerprints?" Tripp asked.

Martin shook his head. "Total zero. Formatted clean."

"Impossible," Overguard spat. "There's always *something* left. A tag, a fragment..."

"Nothing," Martin insisted.

"There's only one answer," Mason said, giving voice to what they all knew but didn't want to admit. "Someone on the inside."

Silence settled on the room, a dark pall. That anyone would give information to The Enemy would have been unthinkable up until the turn of the 20th century. The flip side of the usefulness of technology was the skepticism it inured, enabling The Enemy to work more openly and recruit from sources that would never before have entertained even the possibility. The idea of spiritual warfare had been relegated to the stigma of anti-intellectualism, of the non-scientific. With the rise of the new religion called Science, the supernatural forces that drove the subliminal psyche of humankind paradoxically became even more powerful. The response was a growing fascination in literature and entertainment with the occult and mystical. Evil as an independent force, axiomatic in the past, became an intellectual exercise in psychology. The true nature of humanity, disguised by Science's explanations of everything as random accident, degraded further as The Enemy gained power.

As the illusion of the supremacy of mankind gained converts through the cynical and sterile philosophy of Science, the influence of The Enemy in the lives of ordinary people grew. And as ordinary people increasingly accepted the assertions of The Enemy, it became easier for them to elect or place in power those whose loyalties lay at least indirectly with the Deceiver. This made The Army's task all the more difficult, pitting them against not just The Enemy, but the power structure of humanity itself, increasingly a tool of The Enemy. In short, as humanity lost sight of the fact that there was more to the universe than themselves, that there were things greater than humanity, the more easily The Enemy recruited.

Now, chillingly, it was possible that deception that kept The Enemy in power outside, was penetrating the very ranks of The Army itself. The implications were sobering.

"A new plan needs to be organized, assuming there is a cell working with The Enemy," Martin said. "That means we need to find out exactly who we can trust."

They all nodded their agreement.

"Call the Guild to order," Tripp suggested. "We can start there."

3

E-Yukon and the Guild were both built within the framework of an MMORPG.

Nothing more than a diversion to many and an obsession to some, it was the computer equivalent of an ongoing live theatrical production where the starring roles were given by subscription to ordinary people. For a modest monthly fee, a twelve-year-old girl could become a mighty, invincible, immortal warrior. A ten-year-old boy could vent his animosity against his parents anonymously by harassing people without worrying about the consequences. A sixty-year-old, fat, balding man with a gas problem could become the hero, or heroine, he always wanted to be in life but never found the courage to try to be. A thirty-something woman who never fit into a dress smaller than a size 22 in her life could be a svelte, sexy magician with incredible, high-demand abilities, making her the focus of her combat group, and object of affection, protection, and admiration. It was inevitable that the interactive capabilities intrinsic in the internet should generate this kind of substructure. Within just a few years of the online game's first appearance, the basic design had evolved to the point it was difficult for many, especially the young, to separate their online avatars from their real life.

Virtual reality was fast becoming alternative reality in many ways that profoundly affected reality itself. Early in the process, Mason and his compatriots found certain MMORPGs to be good vehicles for the exchange of information and interaction. Electronic mail, so common as a form of communication, soon showed itself to be too easily susceptible to interception no matter how heavily encrypted or encoded. The complex routing systems that carried the email had too many weaknesses, points easily disrupted or tapped. The MMORPG system, oddly enough, bypassed these problems most efficiently and afforded secure person-to-person communication on a real-time basis. Inside each MMORPG were things called "guilds" or "kinships," where like-minded people signed on together to help each other in the game. These guilds weren't limited by geography or social standing or age or even politics. They very often contained people from 13-70 years of age, all colors, all nationalities, and all backgrounds. Identification of the guild affiliation for a particular player was usually prominently displayed in text about the avatar's image. Mason's cell did not depend only on that, however, as an enterprising hacker could counterfeit that tag easily. There were other, more subtle ways to identify oneself online.

Setting up the system had been a long, tedious task, but the resultant security structure was most rewarding. For over five years, Mason and his cell had participated in the system without a single leak.

Plugged into the MMORPG, Mason, as his avatar Meriack the healer, was traveling to the rendezvous with another North American cell in the virtual city of Ston. He ignored the incessant in-game chatter that scrolled through a yellow-texted window in the lower left-hand corner of his screen. The dirt track displayed as his road stretched toward an eternally blue horizon that magically switched to starry sky as his game clock traded icons from sun to moon. It wasn't a particularly sophisticated online game, but it served its purpose. Changing to one of the newer, prettier and more complex games available would take too long to be worth the trouble at this time. Besides, he wasn't there to enjoy the scenery.

A large animal loomed suddenly before him in the road.

Its appearance didn't alarm Mason. It was, after all, a virtual construct of a grizzly bear presented to occupy his avatar's attention and aid in its advancement through the arbitrary levels of "experience" that equaled success in the game. If he engaged in combat and defeated the bear, his avatar would be given a certain number of points toward a reward of new "abilities". It was part of the game mechanics that drew people to indulge in vicarious violence, satisfying their animal urges and frustrations while giving them a feeling of accomplishment. Mason was not entirely sure it was a healthy way to do things, rewarding violence, however abstract, with such a form of approbation, but he understood the allure. He had felt the same thrill in actual combat, standing over a bleeding, defeated foe. At least this way no one actually suffered, no animal was actually maimed or killed. It was the ultimate sterile, passionless outlet for man's basest instinct: destruction.

There didn't seem to be any way to avoid the belligerent beast, and that annoyed him. His arrival at the rendezvous was going to be delayed by the very programming that protected his team's security and secrecy. Normally, such an encounter ran a certain course. The animal attacked, he counterattacked and in short order would defeat it. The display would briefly announce his victory, points awarded, and the corpse would disappear, allowing him to continue. This would cost him at most a minute or two of inconvenience.

As expected, the bear reared up on its hind legs and opened its mouth to roar. Then things began to go wrong.

"Meriack," the bear said in a computer-generated imitation of a human voice, "turn back!"

Mason hesitated. The bear struck at his avatar four times in quick succession. The avatar's life bar, a green line at the top of the screen, emptied almost immediately. Meriack was dead.

Now, in an MMORPG, when an avatar's life bar zeroed out, the typical series of events led the avatar to fall to its knees and a black screen would appear in the display announcing the unfortunate demise. A grinning skull would then ask if the player wished to continue from the last saved game or quit the game altogether.

The black screen appeared. The skull leered at him and spoke.

"Let this be a warning. We are watching you."

Mason sat stunned as the game shut down.

He didn't care about the death of the avatar. It had died hundreds of times before. What concerned him was the oddity of the events that had just played out. Had their security been breached, or just his identity? He sincerely hoped it was just the latter. That would be a simple fix. The former would mean not just starting anew in another MMORPG, it would require finding a whole new way to communicate. The convenience of the gaming system had enabled the global cells almost instantaneous access, giving them the capability to coordinate strikes against The Enemy on a grand scale. Since its implementation, there had been more victories and progress toward the ultimate goal than in the previous three centuries combined. Loss of use of such a tool would be a crippling blow that would take years, perhaps decades, to recover.

He needed to contact Martin. A few seconds later, they were on the secure land line.

"I don't think it's The Enemy," Martin said in answer to his question. "If The Enemy was behind this breach, at best they would have shut down the system and done something to prevent us rebooting the system."

"And, worst case?"

"They would have tracked us down using the traitor codes and killed us all."

Mason passed a hand across his face and sighed. "Well, then I guess we should be thankful."

Martin was silent on the other end.

"So, someone is on the inside, not The Enemy, not a

traitor?" Mason asked.

"But not friendly, apparently," Martin put in.

Mason agreed with that. Chandler's death was evidence of the lengths to which this mysterious interloper would go. Was one of the other Army cells working against them? Why? What could possibly have been promised that would turn anyone who had seen what The Enemy had truly done to the Earth? If it wasn't another cell, and it wasn't The Enemy...

It was imperative they find out the extent and intent of the breach before any more damage could be done.

* * *

"We've tracked the breach to a particular set of IP's," Martin said.

They were back in E-Yukon, the familiar dryness of the virtual atmosphere echoing the grim air around the table.

"Eastern Europe?" Tripp asked. There was still a vague hope some juvenile hacker was responsible for the puzzle.

Martin shook his head. "Washington, DC."

They sat silent, digesting that information for a moment and considering the implications. There were no friendly cells in America's capital. Since the abandonment of "religious symbols" and moral ideas in preference to political expediency and mercenary ambition, the District of Columbia had become *de facto* Enemy territory.

"No idea which IP exactly?" Overguard pried.

"Not yet," Martin said.

"Does it matter?" Meeker pointed out. "Washington equals Enemy."

"I don't know," Mason interrupted. "We all would be dead, or at least shut down, if that were the case." He stood and went to fidget with the coffee maker. "We're flying blind here. We need information, if we're going to solve this without losing anyone else." He turned to look at them. "Maybe it would be worth it to try to contact them, whoever they are?"

Martin snorted. "Even if we wanted to, and we don't, how would we go about it? We have no way to contact them."

Mason nodded. "True, but I have a feeling it won't be all that hard."

"You think they've penetrated the Guild?" Overguard put in. With his typical cynical gloom, his mind went straight to the worst case scenario.

"They know about my avatar," Mason admitted. "It's a fair bet they deduced any associates are part of The Army." He took a breath before saying it. "Every one of us will be getting a warning soon, I'm sure."

"And when one of us is attacked, we can find out who they are," Meeker finished wryly. "But what do we ask them? If they wanted us to know who they are, wouldn't they've already told us?"

"Maybe they're still not sure they have the right people," Mason ventured.

"Taking a big risk, then, aren't they?" Overguard pointed out.

"Not really," Martin said. "It is a game, after all. A spoken threat from an animated bear? Not so startling to someone outside The Army. Just another part of the game. Odd, yes. Impossible, no."

"Okay," Tripp said. "We need to get a message to the Guild. Somebody needs to arrange a meeting."

* * *

Mason got word from Martin three days later. He called for a meeting inside the game, the only place they were certain would be relatively safe, to advise Mason that contact had been made with a Guild member as expected, but not with one of their cell members. That bothered Mason, but the response to their offer to combine forces had produced something even more disturbing. Their mysterious friend would only meet with one person.

Septimus Vernus. Not Meriack. Not Jonah Mason. Septimus Vernus.

Mason was irritated that the name had been released to the Guild. The majority of them wouldn't know to whom it referred, but his own cell was different. He hadn't told them of much about himself. They knew he was old and that he had been with The Army for a very long time. How long, they probably had not really considered.

"How the heck old are you, anyway?" Martin asked him through his avatar, a warrior named Califor.

"Old enough," Mason answered.

Martin's avatar regarded him placidly, but Mason could see his friend grimacing in his mind's eye.

"Okay, you don't want to talk about it. I get it. But this is a trap, you know."

"I know," Mason replied.

"You sure you want to do this?"

"Want to? No. Have to? Apparently."

"Okay. But you'll be on your own."

Mason chuckled into his headset. "It wouldn't be the

first time, my friend."

Martin's avatar stood quietly immobile for a moment. Mason knew his friend was sitting in front of his keyboard, probably cursing.

"Take care, and stay in touch," Martin finally said.

Mason signed off the game and pulled the I/O set from his neck. Getting free of the device always gave him a sense of relief. Since the latest generation of interface hardware came out, the virtual world had become more intrusive in reality. The addition of scent and personal touch, the simplest beginnings in including the only human senses not previously addressed by game designers, had boosted the effectiveness of the interface devices so much it was impossible to locate the old ones. Mason was one of the last holdouts in using the technologically obsolete equipment, but even his relatively "crippled" I/O made him uncomfortable. Overguard said he was being too paranoid. Mason had laughed at the irony of Overguard telling him that, but inside he wondered if that wasn't true. He had lived so long, seen so much conflict and atrocity; had he become too sensitive to the dark side of human existence? Was he blinded to the better nature of mankind now, poisoned by being witness to so much suffering? There had been good things in his life. He had fathered many children by many lovers. Whole generations in six different countries could trace their ancestry to him, each in a different century and from a different name, of course. Early on he had tried the ruse of posing as his own son or grandson. It had not turned out well. Over the years he'd toyed with different devices to disguise his longevity. He had spent a century or so masquerading as a French count until the whole game had worn thin.

The Enemy might be ruthless, unreasoning, and even occasionally irrational, but they were never boring. Life outside the Conflict, in between engagements, often stretched for years, blindingly routine and mundane. Any readiness exercises or drills had to be carried out in strictest secrecy not only away from The Enemy, but from the world at large. Meetings between the adversaries, which occurred more and more often recently, were increasingly more through the intermediary of the Internet. Virtual meetings sometimes even degenerated into virtual combat. It was appalling to Mason what The Enemy, and even The Army, could do in the real world by the simple insertion of a bit of viral code in a critical junction. Aircraft crashed mysteriously, trains derailed from unknown cause, vital government secrets found their way into hostile hands – so much chaos for so little effort.

All the European cells had weakened significantly

since the fall of Israel in 2037 to Arab forces of the new Persian Empire. The Persians, an alliance of the old nations of Iran, Afghanistan, Iraq and Saudi Arabia, had rolled over the Middle East in a *blitzkrieg* lasting only eight weeks. Egypt sued to enter the Empire in 2038, Turkey shortly thereafter, with the other Middle Eastern nations following suit by 2040. In the decades that followed, refugees of the Empire fled into Russia and Africa. Greece, the Slavic states, and India all struck deals that they knew merely delayed the inevitable.

Mason sighed. He rose and made his way to the bath. He would have to leave the sanctuary of his warded country home. There were specific preparations to be made before venturing into the battlefield.

* * *

The meeting place was a mutually agreed-upon location in a public park. Physical isolation from technological terminals was rare. This place had no telephones, not even cell phone reception. There was no guarantee of shielding from satellite surveillance, but there were ways to blind even the most sophisticated spying resources. Low-tech surveillance posed no immediate threat. High-powered, long-range weaponry was a risk but, again, there were ways to counter that. Mason was not concerned he might fall prey to a sniper or personal explosive device. He had lived too long and weathered too many situations under similar circumstances to worry about physical threat. It was the super-physical, the non-dimensional that concerned him. From that there was always the possibility of the unexpected. That was the real danger.

The park, nestled within the confines of a suburban housing development, bustled with activity. Built around a playground surrounded by an asphalt walking track, the park boasted large stands of poplar and oak from which squirrels and birds scolded the running children. Mothers sat on long benches near the playground, chatting about the latest gossip while keeping a sharp eye on the kids boisterously clambering over the slides, swings, and ladders. The day was bright and blue, a mere hint of clouds moving sedately from west to east. A tiny silver streak raced across their path, the rumble of its jets too faint with distance to be heard over the din of the children. Mason paused for a moment to note the aircraft's flight. It had only been a little over two centuries since men had learned to fly and it still fascinated him.

A familiar tingle and the scent of lilac alerted him to another's presence behind him, but he refused to turn.

"Remarkable things, aren't they?"

Now he did turn to find a well-dressed man in his late forties gazing at the plane as well. "Such a display of man's ability to master the laws of physics, to bind them to his will." He smiled at Mason. He was what one would call handsome in a dark sort of way. Three days growth of beard as black as the hair on his head, piercing green eyes, solidly built from the way his expensive suit clung to him. Mason was not fooled by the jovial demeanor nor by the friendly appearance. This was a Minion of The Enemy. The air of arrogance, the smug confidence of his stance, the hardness in the eyes that belied that smile were all too evident to one who had dealt with his kind for so long.

"I would offer to shake your hand," the man said from behind that grin, "but I'm afraid I might regret it."

Mason was not surprised he'd been so easily spotted. He imagined this man was also well versed in the signs of The Army. Mason nodded his acknowledgment of the man's identity.

"Shall we walk as we talk, then?" Mason suggested.

"Of course."

The man fell into step as Mason set across the park toward the walking path. They strolled in silence for a bit, each taking stock of the other.

"Jonah Mason," the other said last. "An interesting name. Common, yet uncommon. How did you come to choose it?"

Mason shrugged. "It's just a name."

The man chortled. "There's no such thing. We both know that." He looked at the people around him. "Names are controls on things, on people. I speak a name and people react. Some react in recognition, some in curiosity." He stopped abruptly and shouted at a woman walking by. "Rachel?"

The woman paused. She looked at him in puzzlement.

"I'm sorry," the man said. "I thought you were someone I knew."

The woman smiled. "No problem. Have a nice day."

"Thanks. You, too." He watched her walk away a few steps.

Mason caught a heavier scent of lilac as the woman paused again and looked back at them over her shoulder. She smiled and waved.

"Knock it off," Mason said under his breath.

The other gave him an innocent look. "What? Just being friendly."

"You've made your point. Let her go."

With a final grin and a little wave, the man turned away from the woman and caught up to Mason.

"I wasn't going to hurt her," he said. "In fact, she might even like me."

"Stop playing and tell me who you are," Mason snapped as they join the walking track.

"Oh, very well," said the other. "Call me Mike."

"Mike what?"

"Just Mike. It will do for now."

Mason settled into a steady pace, Mike at his side. They moved along the asphalt path past the long bench full of mothers. As they passed from the women's earshot, Mason spoke.

"What do you want from us, Mike?"

"Pardon?"

"You obviously know about the game and several of our identities," Mason said. "Why haven't you used that knowledge?"

"Why, Jonah," Mike said, feigning hurt. "Whatever do you mean? I have no wish to see you harmed."

Mason raised an eyebrow. Mike chuckled.

"All right. Yes, I know about your little system. It's ingenious, I must say. Simple and elegant at once. Still, you must have known it wasn't foolproof. Nothing in this world is."

Mason remained silent. Better to let the man talk. The one failing of The Enemy was its arrogance, its pride in itself. Pressure of speech was common among them, the need to precipitate action by verbal probing. Mason had long understood that tool of theirs and refused to rise to the bait. Mike wanted him to defend the system, to expound on its security and perhaps in that way reveal a weakness. He knew better than to answer that unspoken challenge. After a few moments, Mike nodded his understanding.

"Well," Mike said. "I can see this is going to be more difficult than I expected." He fell quiet for a bit, looking at the children they passed. Several boys were racing around the playground's carousel, laughing. "Have you ever wondered about it, Jonah? The war, I mean. Have you ever wondered why it's still going on after all this time?"

Mason didn't answer, not breaking stride.

"So many people have died in this war. Unnecessarily, I would say. Innocents. Children." He looked at Mason for response. When it became apparent Mason was not going to answer his prodding, he continued. "So many will still die, if it goes on. Family. Friends." They walked for a bit, quietly. "I could do it," Mike went on. "I could tell my masters about the game and you would all die very quickly. Your whole cell would be wiped out in a single day, just like Chandler."

"Yes, you could," Mason agreed. "And you might be right."

"No 'might' about it," Mike said, grinning again.

"So, why don't you?"

Mike dropped to smile at his face turned suddenly hard. "Don't think I won't."

Mason walked on without speaking. They were close now to the heart of the matter, dangerously close. He knew one wrong word could spell disaster, so he kept his face carefully neutral as they paced.

"Your price?" Mason asked.

The smile lit up Mike's face again. "Now you're talking, Jonah, my friend. Now you're talking."

"So, talk to me," Mason said.

Michael rubbed his hands together. "Here's the deal. I'll forget what I know about your little system. In exchange you'll do me a tiny favor."

Mason narrowed his eyes in suspicion at the man.

"Oh, you don't have to worry," Mike said quickly. "I'll not ask you to betray yourselves or any other member of your so-called Army."

"Go on."

"There is a certain faction of our alliance that needs some help in gaining access to information on a person I believe you know. Dorian Azrael."

Mason pulled up short at the name. Warning bells went off in his head. *"Who* did you say?"

Mike spread his hands out, palms upward. It was the sign of neutrality, a reminder of their current status.

"Easy, boy," Mike said, a hard edge back in his voice. "Don't do anything you might regret."

"Dorian Azrael?" Mason repeated. "You must be joking."

"Do I look like I'm joking?" Mike growled.

"Azrael?" Mason said again.

Mike looked around. "Let's walk," he said. "I'll fill you in on the details."

4

"His real name is Azazel," Martin said. He looked around at the rest of the group gathered in the little farmhouse at E-Yukon. "And he works for Dorian Azreal."

An uncomfortable silence settled over the table as they considered that.

"What else do we know about him?" Mason broke the silence.

"Not much that's really significant," Martin went on. "He's a slippery character. Typical Minion. We do know from our Eastern European cells that he was responsible for manufactured information that brought about the downfall of the democratic government of one of South America's larger countries and the installation of a relatively unknown military officer as its new president for life." He paused. "I don't have to tell you which one. The CIA got the fame for that one."

"Go on," Mason encouraged.

"Best we can tell, his headquarters is in Mexico."

Overguard's head snapped up at that. "Where in Mexico?"

"We're not sure," Martin replied. "Somewhere in the Veracruz Province, although he is also associated with Azrael's interests in New York, London, Paris, Berlin, Rome, Rio, Caracas, Lima, and Tokyo."

Overguard leaned back in his chair, scowling. Meeker looked from him to Martin.

"I don't trust him," Janice said.

"Neither do I," Mason replied. "But it's not like we have much choice right now. Until we can work out another secure set of identities, we have to go on."

"I don't like it," Overguard groused. His drawl grew more pronounced in his agitation. "He's making us do his dirty work for him."

"Look at it as just another operation," Martin suggested. "It's not like we haven't pulled similar ops in the past."

"For The Army," Tripp barked. "Not for The Enemy."

"Yeah," Overguard agreed. "This just feels wrong, like we are working for the wrong side."

"Look," Mason said. "Maybe he's running a scam on us, I don't know. But maybe, just maybe, he's actually making a move on Azrael. Can we afford to miss an opportunity like that?"

Nobody spoke up against the idea, he noticed, although everyone still sat frowning nervously. The continual squabbling among The Enemy ranks was well-known. It had afforded them many opportunities in the past to squelch or delay Enemy plans, but it also made them unpredictable.

"Is there a way we can turn this to our advantage, is what I'm trying to say," Mason pressed on. "If there is, we need to be ready to move when the opportunity arises."

Martin sighed and shook his head. "Okay, Mason. You have the lead on this, but what does Azazel want us to do, exactly?"

Mason leaned back in his chair and took a deep breath. "There are certain files on a computer in one of his companies in the Republic of Panama, a list of transactions made between Azrael's agents and a hostile government he's using to blackmail them. Azazel wants them either recovered or destroyed."

"I suppose Azazel is on that list," Tripp said.

Mason shrugged. "Does it matter?"

"It might," Meeker interjected. "If he believes he can

free himself from Azrael's power this way, he must know he could be trading one master for another."

"That may be the idea," Martin said thoughtfully. "He has leverage against us, we will have the same against him. Kind of a standoff."

"Doesn't sound right," Overguard insisted. "No Enemy would accept that kind of deal. He'll double cross us."

"Probably," Mason agreed. "So we need to be extra careful how we handle this. First, we need to start working on a substitute system."

"I have three cells in Asia working on that now," Martin informed them. "There are some very promising oriental systems based on pictography."

"Great. Next, we need to find out how Azazel broke our security."

"We're working backwards from the suspect IPs," Martin reported. "With luck, we'll have the breach identified and corrected within a couple of days."

"Okay," Mason said. "We'll want someone to serve as backup for this op. Second team should be ready to move immediately should first team fail."

"On it," Overguard said. "Best bet is to hit a branch as far as possible from where you go. Germany?"

"Sounds good. That leaves you and me, John," Mason said to Tripp. "You okay with that?"

"I still think this whole thing stinks to high heaven, but I'm with you, boss."

"Right. Let's go over plans."

***

John Tripp had worked with him only twice before. Both times the man performed admirably and courageously. Mason had every confidence he would do so again. It helped that Tripp was a first-class tactician, comparable to any military commander Mason had ever served, although Tripp himself was never in the military. Mason knew Tripp was an American by birth and had lived through the days of Korea, Vietnam, Iraq, and Iran. He wasn't sure, but he suspected Tripp went back even further.

The unspoken agreement among them was that there should be no discussion of their personal lives. The less they knew of each other as individuals, the less chance they would compromise each other should they be captured. It was rare The Enemy took captives, but not unheard of. Not all Enemy forces had the abilities of their leaders. Unlike The Army, which consisted entirely of volunteers, The Enemy troops boasted entire cells of conscripts and mercenaries. These quickly fell apart when their leader was eliminated. Loyalty to the goal, a prime tenet of Army volunteers, was rare in even the highest echelons of The Enemy and that, more than anything else, kept the Conflict going so long. A large portion of the intelligence gathered against The Enemy came from double agents and converts. The Enemy, though they knew of the presence of spies, rarely tried to hide their plans, another manifestation of their arrogance, often a costly one. Mason had seen more than one Enemy operation go sour that way, at an appalling cost of human life. The great wars of the 19th and 20th centuries were only the latest and most blatant examples. If it weren't for the fertility and fecundity of the human race, the Conflict would have long before been reduced to its principal combatants.

On bad days, Mason would gloom over the seeming injustice of it all. Why did the Master let it go on? What possible purpose did He see in all the suffering? Mason, bloody handed on the battlefields of Anatolia, Tripoli and Tunisia, Constantinople and the Khyber Pass, had asked that question to the accompaniment of the cries of the wounded and dying.

Still, he was a soldier in the Cause. He had to have faith in the justice of his Master. As he had fought for the glory and love of Rome all those years ago, he fought for the glory and love of a higher calling. The end would come someday, in his lifetime or afterward. He was a cog in the great machine, a position he cherished. It gave him personal purpose, a reason to live, which was more than many people ever had. Sometimes he wondered if that was why the Conflict continued: to give them, The Army and The Enemy, a reason to live. There certainly seemed precious little other reason.

Their target company was Catalina Industries, headquartered in Panama City, Panama. They could have used their resources on the Internet to hack into the company's files, but that would have posed a threat to their own systems. Just as Martin's team was backtracking their security breach, following a faint electronic trail with the tenacity of technological bulldogs, The Enemy could likewise uncover their interference and further damage their network integrity. To prevent such an event, Mason and Tripp traveled to Panama under assumed names, taking accommodations at one of the city's older hotels, El Ejecutivo. The rooms were spare but comfortable, and only a few blocks from Catalina's office building.

Panama, only a few degrees off the equator, was a country where the myriad hues of green reflected from the rainforest were broken intermittently by a burgeoning and fast spreading urban landscape of concrete and glass. Since the US abandoned claim on the Panama Canal at the turn of the 21st century, the presence of Chinese and Cuban companies had exploded. Even the brief popularity of the western interior provinces to American and European retirees had not slowed the country's expanding dependency on eastern money.

Panama City itself was indistinguishable from hundreds of other urban complexes throughout Central and North America. High-rise apartment buildings crowded to the shore of Panama Bay, facing the Pacific where Taboga Island hugged the coast line and farther out the Contadora Islands harbored mansions for dignitaries from many countries. Within the modern perimeter of banks and office buildings, universities and hospitals, government bureaus and municipal projects, the ruins of Old Panama still stood. Reduced by the pirate Henry Morgan's wrath and the weather of centuries to an empty stone tower and a shadow of its frame and shattered foundation, Panama Viejo endured, a monument to the time when The Enemy was not so strong, when men still remembered their true Master, no matter how twisted that memory had become from over 1500 years of the Conflict.

It was there, standing within the destroyed walls of that place, that Mason and Tripp finalized their plans. The operation was simple and direct. Complex plans had too many ways to fail. They would arrange for an appointment with a minor functionary in the company headquarters, disable him and use his office computer to finish the job. Azazel had provided them with a USB drive containing passwords and software to quickly bypass the company safeguards. A few seconds connected to any station would be sufficient to download the files Azazel wanted. He had also included a virus on the little drive that would destroy the resident files, leaving only the stolen files behind.

Tripp had convinced Martin to carry that virus one step further. The one on the USB drive now would not only destroy the resident files, but carried a nasty surprise. The result would leave no doubt that the system had been compromised, but Mason had no reason to hide the internal hack. He actually hoped that the destruction of the files would be discovered, after they have escaped of course. With any luck, and a few well placed hints, Azazel would be blamed, since he would be most likely to benefit from the crime. The Enemy was very unforgiving of traitors. Best case scenario, they would kill two birds with one stone.

Posing as buyers for a Canadian construction firm, they soon found themselves ushered past building security to the visitors' waiting room. Their appointment was with one M. Valdez, Associate Vice President of Sales. The M. turned up to stand for Maria, which annoyed Mason and amused Tripp. Mason disliked The Enemy's use of women in vulnerable positions, although he could understand the psychology. It was the same reason Middle Eastern terrorists based their operations out of hospitals, schools, and holy places. They had no real respect for those locations, but knew their opponents must, or go against the very values they were supposed to protect. The Enemy never allowed themselves to be drawn into what could be called a "fair fight." Why should they? It wasn't who they were, after all.

Ms. Valdez' space was on the third floor. It wasn't so much an office as a cubicle ensconced in a row of similar cubicles, all announcing their occupants as "Associate Vice President" of this or that. It became immediately clear some improvisation was going to be required if the operation was to succeed. Mason was undaunted. The old adage about no plan ever surviving first contact with the enemy was well known to him.

Ms. Valdez was in her late 30s, very professional and meticulous. Her workstation was a testimony to her fastidiousness in dress and behavior. Her computer, blank except for a password window, was set back in a tiny desktop free of the clutter associated with pictures of family or hobbies. Mason deduced the job was her life, another annoyance, as what they must do would surely result in her removal, if not worse.

"We are very glad you've chosen Catalina for your project," she began as she opened her computer desktop, deftly blocking their view of the password with her body as she took her own seat. Mason noticed she had entered only two keys and surmised she had a longer password partially entered already. He admired her caution.

"Yes, well, Catalina came highly recommended," Tripp said. "Pantano and Marshall Enterprises spoke very highly of your services."

The name, carefully selected from published records, obviously meant nothing to her, but she smiled anyway.

"It's always nice to find that our customers think well enough of us to pass along our name," she said. Her English, except for the softest accent, was as perfect as her hair and taste in jewelry. A single, simple gold cross hung from a tiny gold chain around her neck. "Now, I understand you have some requisitions to discuss?"

Mason lifted his briefcase from the floor. "May I?" he asked, indicating her desk.

"Please," she said, shifting farther back into the cubicle

to allow him room.

"The papers I have simply require signatures," Mason began. He went on with his rehearsed speech as he opened the case. Lifting a folder out of the case, he handed it to her. As she took it, she gasped and snatched her hand away.

"I'm terribly sorry," Mason said with concern. "This ring of mine seems to be always in the way."

She smiled and shook her head. "No, no. It's only a scratch. Please, don't worry about it." She stopped and shook her head again. "Don't worry about it."

"Go," Mason told Tripp.

Tripp reached around Ms. Valdez and shoved the flash drive into the computer USB port.

"Forty seconds," Mason reminded him.

"Don't worry about it," Valdez reassured him.

"What she said," Tripp grinned. "Virus uploading."

"Don't worry about it."

"Thirty seconds."

"Done," Tripp said. He pulled the flash drive from the USB port and slipped it back into the secret pocket in his boot.

"Please," Mason said directly to Valdez as her eyes refocused. "Let me apologize over lunch."

Ms. Valdez turned back to her computer. "I'm not sure

that would be appropriate," she said stiffly. "If you'll just read me your requisition number..."

"Of course," Mason apologized. "You are quite right. Let's stick to business."

**

"The drug should be wearing off shortly," Tripp said as they left the building, quickening his step.

"Well, it will still be a bit before she remembers everything," Mason said. "By then, we'll be in Costa Rica."

"Too bad," Tripp mourned. "I wanted to visit the old Fort Portobello."

"And I wanted to see the Golden Altar again, but that's not going to happen either."

They caught the bus to the Tocumen Airport outside the city. Using Austrian passports, they flew into San Jose before dark. From there, they made their way home in a more leisurely pace. On the plane back to the States, Mason allowed himself a few moments of guilt for what they had done. He never felt that way in combat. There it was kill or be killed, a true black-and-white matter of survival. On the technological battlefield things were not so well defined. There was collateral damage in any conflict, as he knew, but that did nothing to salve his conscience at times like this. The only redeeming factor to this operation was it allowed his cell and the cells closest to them to continue operations, retaining them and their resources for use against The Enemy. One life lost or destroyed to save many. Never an easy choice, and too often a necessary one.

A light tone came over the plane's PA, followed by the attendant advising them of landing procedures. Mason sighed and buckled his belt, turning his attention now to what they could do with the information they had gleaned. Martin's virus was built to fool or bypass any known anti-virus software. Since it was entered directly into the mainframe, it could be as much as a week before it got traced to Valdez' station. If she was smart and reported the incident before IT security found it, she might get off with a reprimand. Mason hoped she was smart. If not, well, collateral damage.

"How long before Azazel knows, you think?" Tripp asked as they waited by the baggage claim.

Mason shrugged. "A day? A week? An hour? He might know already." Mason snagged his suitcase as it went by on the belt. "I assume he has a way of monitoring the files."

Tripp grinned wickedly. "I hope so. That virus can do very nasty things to computers."

Mason laughed. "Stop it. You're frightening me."

"It does," Tripp insisted.

"I believe you," Mason told him. "I'm just not sure you should enjoy it so much."

Tripp mumbled something about Boy Scouts and turned away to grab his own bag. Mason grinned to himself.

"So, what do you think about Overguard and Meeker?" Tripp asked as they rolled their luggage toward the exit.

"What about them?"

Tripp snorted. "You do know they're a couple."

Mason paused as the doors slid open with a sigh and the sounds of traffic grew. He turned to his friend. "What?"

"You amaze me, Mason," Tripp said with a chuckle. "For somebody with your rep for sharp observation, you can be really blind to some things." He led Mason through the doors and stopped at the curb to hail a cab. "Who do you think recruited Meeker?"

"I assumed..." Mason stopped. What had he assumed? He had recruited Martin and Tripp himself, but who had recruited Overguard? He didn't know. Overguard had come to them from a southern cell that lost most of its members in a particularly nasty encounter during the early years of the Cold War. He had come highly recommended by Central, and

Mason had never thought to challenge that judgment. Perhaps he should have. If Overguard had recruited Meeker without consulting him, what else had he done on his own?

"Yeah, well, you know what they say about 'assume,'" Tripp said as the taxi pulled up.

"How do you know all this?"

Tripp shook his head. "Don't you ever just have a conversation any more, man?"

"We're not supposed to know too much about each other," Mason replied.

"You trust us with your life, Mason. Doesn't it make sense you should know *something* about us?" He handed his bag to the driver and reached to open the cab door. "Overguard wanted to go to Germany because Meeker lives in Berlin. I think he probably thought he could kill two birds with one stone, as it were."

Mason gave him a hard look, to which Tripp only responded with a wide grin.

"Want to know where Overguard lives?" Tripp smirked. "Amsterdam."

***

Azazel did indeed know about it by the time they signed into E-Yukon. Martin met them on the front porch swing. The old dog was nowhere to be found. Mason realized it was the first time he'd been missing.

"Where's the dog?" he had to ask.

Martin grimaced. "Written out. We traced the breach to an IP that had access to its subroutine and piggybacked a key logger. It was registered to Catalina Industries."

"What?" Tripp blurted. "You mean that *we* were the leak that they used to get Chandler?"

"Essentially, yes," Martin said. "Sucks, huh?"

"But how did they get access to the server to use the code?" Mason asked.

"We're working on that. By the way, we got another message from Mike."

"Really?" Mason said unenthusiastically.

"He sends his thanks and congratulations on job well done." Martin said with a grin. "He wanted to know if there was any way to do it without crashing the company database, though."

"Probably," Tripp spoke up. "But where's the fun in that?"

Martin laughed.

"Anything else?" Mason interrupted.

"No, why?"

Mason frowned. "No other demands? Threats?"

Martin shook his head. "No. It is odd, now that I think about it. I've been so focused on plugging the leaks..."

Mason looked around. "Overguard? Meeker?"

There was a long pause as they exchanged worried looks. They all jumped when a voice spoke from the screened doorway.

"I'm here," Meeker said. "But I'm afraid we may have lost Overguard."

5

"Overguard called me from Amsterdam after connecting up with the London office," Martin said. "I was so busy coordinating the security investigation, I didn't have time to talk to him very long. I suggested he contact Janice."

"He did," Meeker said. "He told me he was headed to Berlin with one of the London contingent as backup. If things went badly in Panama, they would try in the German office."

"It would be a little more difficult to access the Panamanian files from there, but it would be harder to detect their activity," Martin explained.

"Right. But, after he checked in with me when he got to Berlin, I didn't hear from him," Meeker said, worriedly. "That's not like him. I thought that maybe London might have heard from their man, so I called them," Meeker told them as they sat grimly listening. The little dingy table looked more gray than usual and the air was particularly dry. "They haven't heard anything either."

"We should go to Berlin," Tripp said.

"No," Mason stopped him. "Overguard knew the risks. We have to rely on him to get out of this on his own."

"He's one of us," Tripp snapped. "We owe it to him to try, at least."

"London is closer," Martin put in. "We'll ask them."

"I already did," Meeker smiled. "That team was dispatched this morning."

Tripp subsided, still glaring at Mason.

"If he can be found, London will find him," Mason assured them. "We need to concentrate on other problems. There is still a matter of how the server was hacked and by whom."

"We're making real progress there," Martin said. "The source should be identified by this time tomorrow."

"Great," Mason said. "Then, let's work on the new security system. We can't rely just on the game anymore. Suggestions?"

"How about a simple intranet?" Tripp said.

"Would that be any more secure than regular Internet connections?" Meeker asked.

Martin nodded. "Our South African cells have been working on a system based on a megabit encryption developed to protect the diamond trading databases. Not exactly the same, of course, but with that for a foundation and the resources of the rest of The Army, a new intranet should serve admirably."

"How long will it take to boot?" Mason asked.

"Four, five days at the most."

Mason frowned. "A long time."

"Yeah. Sometimes I miss the good old days," Tripp commented. "Back when getting a letter in three days was considered fast."

"Soldier up, John," Mason said with a grin.

Tripp grunted in answer.

Martin jumped in. "We just got a message from Mike. He wants to meet and discuss negotiations."

Mason exchanged looks with Tripp and Meeker. As uncomfortable as the situation had been, it was about to get considerably worse. How they dealt with Azazel could mean the difference between life and death. Their strong point was possession of the files that, in Azrael's hands, had controlled Azazel's power. Exactly how or why was something they'd had no chance to explore. On the other hand, Azazel knew about their online communications system, and they had no idea how long he'd been inside, what he'd discovered, or whether he had committed a further mischief than the dog.

They were whistling in the dark, and the worst part was the time limit. Mason only hoped those files were so critical Azazel would be willing to make a deal that would give them enough time to isolate themselves from the network. If Mason and his associates had to die, at least the rest of the cells would be protected. That Azazel came to him for the job, to his enemy rather than his allies, said volumes about his need to make those files disappear and that he not be implicated.

The Enemy's Minions feared very little. What they did fear most was the attention of their superiors. As long as their actions didn't affect those above them, they had a free hand. Immune to human authority, legal or illegal, they indulged themselves in every vice, from drugs to murder. Eventually, one might say inevitably, their indulgences overlapped. When the overlap was between Minions of equal rank, there were usually no repercussions. In this case, Mason had a good idea that Azazel had overstepped his bounds somehow. Finding out how, exactly, would give them a stronger position from which to negotiate.

"Where and when?" Mason asked.

"Same place. Now."

That Azazel wanted a meeting immediately said that he knew every hour The Army was in possession of those files brought them closer to that answer. They needed to stall, delay the meeting as long as possible without forcing Azazel to use his own trump card.

"Tell him no," Mason answered.

"No?" Martin repeated.

"He won't release his information until he's sure we can't retaliate," Mason explained.

"Standoff," Tripp nodded.

"I don't know," Meeker said. "Sounds kind of dangerous to me. Maybe we could at least hear what he's offering." She shrugged. "Would we be any worse off?"

"We've dealt with them more than I like already," Mason told her.

"She may have a point, Mason," Tripp said. "And it might give us just the time we need."

Mason looked at each of his colleagues in turn. Martin looked distracted, probably processing incoming information. Tripp and Meeker both waited for his decision with an air of deference. He had come to accept the fact, early on in the formation of their cell, he had gravitated into the position of leader. Although Martin was the heart of the cell, its cord with other cells and point of contact with outside entities, Mason was its head. He suspected it was because they knew he was the oldest among them. The fact he had survived all this time in a Conflict that taken so many lives was no mean feat, and they respected him for that. True, there were older veterans who, like Mason, had gained the nickname Angelkillers. Mason took no delight being called that. It reminded him of too much. The nickname was an unofficial title given to those who had been a part of the Conflict more than 1000 years. It made him feel his age when he heard it. The weight of the centuries sat almost as heavily on him as the responsibility of leadership.

Finally, he sighed. Tripp was right. Anything to delay the inevitable was to their advantage. It was just a matter of how long the situation could be drawn out before something snapped.

"All right," he said. "John, can you be there?"

"Sure, if you want."

"I want. Janice, keep after London. We need to find Overguard."

"On it," she promised.

"Let's do this," Mason said, and logged off.

***

It was late afternoon. The park, unlike before, was almost empty. The lengthening shadows formed dark thoughts in his mind as Mason strode with Tripp toward the rendezvous point.

The scent of lilac brought Mason up short. Tripp broke stride and turned.

"What is it?" he asked.

Mason frowned, silencing Tripp with a hand signal. Tripp looked nervously around, his hand reaching to the .38 he carried at his shoulder. Mason hardly noticed his discomfort. He was trying to locate the source of that aroma. Years of confrontation with The Enemy had taught him that the scent of lilac was all the warning you sometimes got before things went wrong. He had tried to explain that to the others in the cell, but they seemed incapable of smelling it. Mason eventually concluded it was something in himself, an awareness they did not share, that gave him the ability to sense the lilac.

Tripp moved closer to him and pulled his weapon, checking it for load. His movement disrupted Mason's concentration. The lilac scent faded.

"Stand still!" Mason snapped.

Tripp froze.

A few feet from them a ripple appeared in the air. Mason

growled as Azazel stepped into existence, but there was more.

Azazel had forgotten who he faced. With centuries of combat under his belt, facing every kind of Enemy along the way, Mason's senses were honed to catch the tiniest hint of deceit. He sensed rather than saw the two beings still in the rift behind Azazel.

"Hello, Angelkiller," Azazel said with a smirk. "That is what they call you, isn't it?" He glared at Tripp. "What exactly do you plan doing with that?"

To his credit, Tripp didn't flinch. He grinned. "Just a little target practice."

Azazel turned back to Mason. "This is supposed to be a friendly meeting," he said. "You brought a bodyguard?"

Mason didn't counter that one. He barked a command and compelled the two Minions behind Azazel to manifest, then sealed the rift with another word. Inside the rift, they were protected. Now they were as physical as Mason and Tripp, perhaps for the first time. They were definitely disoriented. Azazel hissed angrily, trying to reopen the rift.

"Shoot," Mason ordered.

Tripp raised his weapon.

"Wait!" Azazel shouted, throwing up his hands in surrender.

The .38 sounded like a cannon in the quiet afternoon air. One of Azazel's lieutenants crumpled. The other dropped to the ground and covered his head in terror. A bloodcurdling howl rose from the dying lieutenant. The .38 spoke again, cutting off the wail abruptly. Tripp lowered his weapon at the second man.

"Wait, dammit!" Azazel yelled again.

Another shot and another wail voiced, fading quickly into nothing. The bodies, motionless, flickered briefly, then passed from existence into the nothing from which they had spawned.

Azazel cursed in several different languages until he realized the .38 was trained on him. He fell silent, his face blanching as he looked at the weapon.

"Impossible!" he managed at last.

"Apparently you are mistaken," Tripp grinned again.

Azazel glowered at him, deep hatred in his eyes. "You are dead," he told Tripp. "You will suffer greatly for what you have done."

"Enough," Mason said, stepping forward. "He is under my protection."

"Then it is *you* who will suffer," Azazel growled, turning on him. "Your master frowns on murder."

"Casualties of war," Mason corrected. "They were yours

to protect. You could've stepped in front of the bullets, taken the consequences of your deceit upon yourself."

"My deceit?"

"I have dealt with your kind many times in the past," Mason said. "Such an ambush is too obvious."

"I came to make a deal!" Azazel protested.

"And so you shall," Mason answered. "However, in my version of the story, my colleague and I survive the negotiation."

"I will not negotiate at the point of a gun," Azazel said, recovering himself.

"Then, there will be no negotiations," Mason announced. "You can leave the way you came, or the way your men did."

"Wait," the other said, holding out his hands palms upward. "Let's start again. We can discuss this reasonably, can't we? You have something on me, I have something on you. Let's talk."

Mason waited for a few moments before responding. He watched Azazel closely for any further sign of deceit. The scent of lilacs faded at last.

"Very well," he said when the air blew clearly to the nearby trees once more.

"I admit I was a bit overzealous about my security," Azazel cooed. "I apologize for not trusting your intentions. It's just that I'm not used to dealing with such upright gentlemen as yourselves."

"Skip it," Mason snapped. "Get to the point."

Azazel's grin was quick, but stopped short of his eyes, which blazed hotly.

"The point," he said, "is that I want those files, all of them, including any copies you have made, destroyed."

"That much we already knew," Mason responded.

"Of course," Azazel went on. "Name your price. You want wealth? I can guarantee your little army funding to keep it going indefinitely. Power? How about a presidency? I can see to it you're set for life as head of just about any country you choose, within reason.

"But perhaps you are more interested in helping your fellow man. What would you say to the establishment of a humanitarian foundation to feed the world's poor? Or how about an organization dedicated to finding the cure for cancer? Those are always so beneficial – and profitable to boot."

"Here's what we want," Mason countered. "You will swear before your master and mine to never divulge the information you have concerning us."

At the mention of his master, Azazel flinched, his eyes shifting back and forth nervously.

"Be careful how you speak," Azazel said. "Words have power, you know."

"I did know," Mason replied. "That is why you are to swear by your —"

"Stop!" Azazel snapped, holding up his hand to silence Mason. "I heard you the first time."

Mason and Tripp waited as Azazel pondered. Mason could almost see the man's mind at work, weighing the pros and cons, turning over the implications in his mind.

Dealing with The Enemy was always a gamble. Sometimes they actually kept their word, though more often than not it was because to go back on it would cause harm to themselves. The Minions were famous for deception and double dealing — it was their stock in trade, again. Mason no more trusted Azazel than his master, but by making him swear to that master and Mason's own, he hoped Azazel would be sufficiently bound to comply. Of course, if the man was rogue enough to move against Azrael, it was possible even such a dire oath would mean little to him. It was a risky proposition, one Mason did not make likely. He fully expected Azazel to demand a similar oath from him, one, should he agree, he would be bound to honor. They were down to the wire, and there would be little time to find the answers they needed once the deal was struck. Mason only hoped they had stalled long enough.

"Your deal is acceptable on one condition," Azazel said at last.

Mason steeled himself for what he was sure would come. He was prepared to give his word, to honor it and take the consequences. Just negotiating with The Enemy was frowned upon by his Master. It inferred power to The Enemy, however obliquely, that they did not deserve. Mason was not sure why the Master had allowed them to get to this point, but he had faith the Master was working a plan that led to eventual victory. War, like politics, made strange bedfellows, and sometimes compromise was the best way to avoid bloodshed. Tripp, Meeker, Martin, and Overguard were his responsibility. He was willing to go a long way to see to their safety, but it would have its price. You eventually have to stand before the Master and justify your actions. He set his jaw and looked Azazel in the eye.

"What is it?" he asked.

"A hostage," Azazel said from behind the hard eyed grin. "Until I'm sure of your compliance, I will hold one of your team hostage. When I am sure, the prisoner will be released."

It took only a second for Mason to recover from the shock.

"Unacceptable," he said.

Azazel's smile vanished, leaving only the grim demeanor, now completely unveiled.

"I thought you might say that," he said. The air around them crackled, wavered, and he snapped out of existence.

A few seconds ticked by.

"Well," Tripp said, "that could have been worse."

Mason shook his head. "This isn't over, not by a long shot."

The scent of lilac burst over them. The air all around rippled and snapped.

"Here they come," Mason warned. "Remember your wards."

"Don't worry about me, boss," Tripp said, reloading his weapon.

They stood back to back as the enemy attacked. Mason, the calm of battle spirit settling on him, noted there were only ten opponents. Had Azazel once more underestimated them? Had the Minion's arrogance seen their willingness to negotiate as weakness? Or was Azazel only testing them, playing with their resolve? Perhaps he thought a simple show of force would do to convince them that they should surrender and beg for terms.

The sun set as the enemy troops circled. They had chosen

not to appear in human form. Mason wasn't sure what Tripp saw, for each person perceived The Enemy differently. Where Mason saw the winged and taloned demons of his own time's interpretation, Tripp probably saw more refined but equally malefic images. He gave no more than an instant's consideration to the puzzle as he reached into his coat to produce the runed dirk he carried for just such a contingency.

He welcomed this fight. It was familiar, primal. Kill or be killed. A grim smile spread over his face. Adrenaline coursed through him as the enemy charged.

Tripp's weapon spoke behind him, but Mason barely heard it over the thundering of his own heart in his ears. Three enemy closed on him, their black talons outstretched. He barked a word of rebuke, stunning one. The second caught his dirk in its throat, a quick thrust and twist to free the weapon and slash at the third. As the wounded one fell back, coughing blood and crumbling to the ground, he felt the dirk sink into the other's chest. He spun, the dagger coming free again, a dark spray of demon blood following its arc. He found himself facing two more. Two gunshots told him Tripp was still up.

The enemy fell back. Rather than separate, the men returned to their ready position, back-to-back.

"Count?" He shouted over the wail of the wounded.

"Two dead, one down," Tripp replied.

"One dead, one down," Mason reported.

"Getting old?" Tripp jibbed.

The enemy charged again. Mason was sure now they had orders to kill and would not relax. There was no art to their attack. They simply strove to overpower. It was almost a foregone conclusion they would lose, but they didn't know that. Tripp's weapon barked twice.

The stunned one was too slow to fend off this thrust. The other two closed, trying to get inside his defense while he was dispatching the first. A quick turn of the blade, a twist of his wrist and another fell, blood spurting from its throat. The last one, hindered by the falling body of its comrade, couldn't avoid Mason's stroke.

The aroma of death hung heavily around them, masking the fading lilac scent. Mason checked with Tripp before lowering his own guard. His friend was scanning the park around them, weapon at the ready.

"We need to go before the local LEOs get here," Mason said.

Tripp nodded grimly as they watched the enemy corpses dissolve.

"One thing I'll say about them: they're tidy," Tripp

commented, tucking the weapon back into its holster.

"We've just inconvenienced Azazel is all," Mason said as he stowed his knife. The blade shone clean in spite of the combat. "He knew we could take them. He just wanted us to know he was unhappy with us."

Tripp grunted. "Unhappy? How many will he throw at us when he's full-blown pissed?"

Mason shot his friend a meaningful look. "Time to check in," he said.

***

Truth be told, Tripp both enjoyed and dreaded Mason's company. The man was so blasted intense about everything it got annoying if they were together for an extended period. He reminded Tripp of Lion Gardiner sometimes, who he'd known so very long ago. Like Gardiner, Mason had a soldier's understanding of life. Other times Mason reminded him of one of the Mathers brothers. They'd had the same humorless attitude about life. His own Puritan background had never seemed to purge his sense of fun and the ridiculous. Not that *that* hadn't bought him its fair share of trouble, but, what the heck?

Things were definitely simpler back then. The biggest worry the settlement had was the Pequot Indians and whether or not the colony would last the next winter. Maybe it wasn't healthy to dwell on the past, but he had good memories of those days, and he wasn't going to give those up for anything. Mason offered him an excuse to leave the mundane surroundings of his Connecticut home for adventure of the highest order.

Money was not an issue for him. His family's wealth was rooted in investments made years before his grandfather was born. Not having to worry about his finances gave Tripp a freedom few people had, but he wasn't really interested in taking advantage of that. He was more interested in being faithful to his duty, and so he channeled all his resources into his Army cell's operations. None of the others ever evidenced any curiosity as to where the funds came from to maintain their operations, and that was fine with Tripp. He knew too many sycophants in his role as executor of his family estate. He admired Mason because the man never seemed to change, never got his jokes, never rose to his jibes. From the first time he met Mason, the man's manner had fascinated him.

It was the spring of 1721 and he had just ridden into New York on family business. The trip from Saybrook was long and tiring. He wanted to find a boarding house, have a bath and a shave and a good night's sleep in a real bed. He was considering what to do to celebrate his 59th birthday, sitting before the fireplace in the boarding house with a brandy and his pipe, when Mason had come in and sunk into the chair opposite.

They had exchanged pleasantries and then sat silently contemplating the flames for several minutes. Tripp was struck by Mason's gaze into the fire. He got the impression there was something bothering the man. His interest piqued, he asked the question that probably prompted everything that followed.

"Is there something I can do to help?"

Why he'd asked it that way remained a mystery, but from that moment he and Mason formed a fast friendship. Of course, his name hadn't been John Tripp then. Nor was Mason's the same. They had both gone through many changes since, and though they were vastly different in temperament, that difference only seemed to strengthen their connection.

He found Mason's seemingly imperturbable manner refreshing, and he soon realized that what he had taken for anxiety there in front of that boarding house fireplace was actually an intensity of concentration that manifested whenever Mason was contemplating a particularly complex problem.

It turned out that Mason was in New York pursuing a

particularly evasive opponent. Mason's candid discussion of his problem intrigued Tripp and, more out of curiosity than anything else, he agreed to get involved.

He never regretted that decision. He only wished he'd met Mason years earlier.

6

Martin glared at the computer screen accusingly. It glared back at him stubbornly, the display announcing that once again he was denied access.

"Come *on*," he muttered. "Give it up, already."

He rubbed his eyes, sighing. The computer clock said he had been working for six hours straight. No wonder he was hungry. Reluctantly, he logged off and disconnected the CPU. It wouldn't do to have his system hacked while he wasn't at the keyboard to defend himself.

He checked the refrigerator. Peanut butter? What was that doing there, behind the milk? Oh, yeah. Breakfast had been interrupted by an inspiration that, unfortunately, had not panned out. He pulled the jar out and placed it by the breadbasket where it belonged. Another foray into the refrigerator brought ham and cheese to the table. The bag of potato chips came down out of the pantry to empty its last contents on to his plate. He grumbled to himself about the few remaining slices of bread. Time to hit the grocery again. Such was the life of a bachelor. Feed when hungry. Travel when necessary.

He was so glad to have The Army to fill out his time away from work. The computer company was becoming a real bore. Their latest advances were so far behind The Army's it was comical. It was a relief to come home to his own equipment, which used a fraction of the electricity and produced an order of magnitude more results than all the hardware in his lab.

Still, the security leak evaded his best efforts. Whoever his opponent was, they had at least a comparable skill to his own, and that really worried him. Mason and the others depended on him to locate and plug the leak. That was a serious responsibility he did not take lightly. He couldn't fail them. There was too much at stake.

He owed it to Mason at least. The man had taken him in when he had been ready to give up. His native Germany had turned on humanity, to his shame. They had attacked without provocation, rationalizing their aggression by the flimsiest of excuses. So what if some Austrian Archduke got assassinated? Did that justify invasion? Did it excuse murder on a massive scale?

He met Mason at a Philadelphia train station in early 1915. They hit it off at once, talking about the futility of war and the waste of human life for a few thousand acres of land. Their friendship had deepened over the next two years, but it wasn't until that day in 1918 when Mason first spoke of The Army that he realized the man had been vetting him for recruitment.

Mason showed him a way of looking at the war in Europe that explained why things happened as they did, not in the weak and contrived way the national leaders used, but in the true and obvious. Through Mason, he came to understand so much more about the world that he forgot himself and his own petty concerns. But no matter how Mason may have given him a new way of looking at the world, it was his own research in universities and libraries around the world that would convince him of the truth of that vision.

He became aware.

He uncovered the scope of the Conflict through that research, tromping through archeological digs between the wars, interviewing people who witnessed events firsthand rather than depending on academic and media reports. It had cost him precious time and much personal expense, but before he committed to what Mason suggested, he had to satisfy himself of its truth.

Unbeknownst to Mason, he traced the man's personal history back an incredible five hundred years without break. He suspected Mason went even further back, probably over a thousand years, but records before the sixteenth century were too sparse to follow. Now this name, Septimus Vernus? His respect for Mason grew the more he discovered about the man. How do you argue with the statements of someone who had seen that much? Had lived that long? And, when what that person tells you is confirmed again and again by independent sources, when do you stop questioning?

Martin became supremely confident Mason was for real. He had no doubts the man was telling the truth, and that scared him. For months, he debated whether to join this resistance Mason had invited him to join.

Then the bombs fell on Hiroshima and Nagasaki.

Whether or not the attacks were justified was immaterial to him. That things had come to such a state, that was what was important. Conventional warfare was one thing, but this was something frightening in its implications. He suspected many people, similarly alarmed, came to be recruits for The Army in those days. A new and terrifying chapter had opened in human history, one so blatantly precipitated by The Enemy it could not be denied.

A knock at the door pulled him from his thoughts. He carried the sandwich with him as he answered it.

"Harold Martin?" the messenger with the clipboard asked.

"Yes?"

***

E-Yukon was down. Mason tried for more than fifteen minutes to log in before going to the secure land line. Martin didn't answer. After redialing twice, he abandoned that channel as well. There was only one recourse. He would have to physically visit Martin.

Last he knew, Martin lived near Philadelphia. It was possible the man had moved, but Mason doubted it. Martin was the kind that spent most of his time working with computers, and very little else. Once he had established himself in the computer company, he would probably have settled in wherever he was and concentrated on developing and improving The Army's systems. It only made sense to start there and only then, if necessary, use Army resources to track him.

A physical visit was dangerous, possibly disastrous. If he was followed or tracked somehow, he could be leading The

Enemy directly to the cell's hub. Martin controlled E-Yukon and coordination with other cells. Of all of them, his position was most critical. The security surrounding him was very tight, as much as they could manage. The thought that he might be out of commission, dead, or otherwise, was a real blow to the cell.

He had just finished packing when the secure line buzzed. He hurried to answer, sinking into the chair by the phone.

"Martin!" He said, unable to hide the relief in his voice.

"Nope, just me," Overguard's voice replied.

"Steve? Where have you been?"

"What do you mean?"

"You were supposed to check in hours ago," Mason accused.

"What you talking about? I called Janice," Overguard answered.

A cold chill went down his back.

"Mason? What's going on? I can't raise Martin," Overguard went on. "London's not answering either."

"Are you still in Berlin?"

"Yes, why?"

"Get out," Mason nearly shouted. "Get out now. Head to Rome HQ. Don't pack, just go."

"On my way."

The line went dead. Mason sank into a nearby chair and allowed himself a single curse.

Of course, he thought. Why hadn't he seen it? Someone inside had to have given Azazel access to E-Yukon code. Martin was too well protected. Overguard wasn't versed enough in computers. Tripp was fiercely loyal to The Army. But Meeker...

What did he know about her? They had deliberately avoided meeting in person for security reasons. He knew her only through E-Yukon. As far as he knew, only Overguard had ever met her. And everyone in E-Yukon was a mere avatar, a computer-generated character remotely controlled by a cell member hundreds, sometimes thousands of miles away. Physical distance was irrelevant in cyberspace.

Who was actually controlling the Meeker avatar? He unwrapped a Montecristo and moistened the end. Snipping it open, he set the cigar between his teeth.

The dog had been a decoy to draw a Martin out, to get him to expose himself. It was a fair bet Martin was gone, and that meant the cell was neutralized to all intents and purposes. He chewed on the smoke in frustration.

They were dead in the water. He had Overguard and Tripp, but no real secure way to contact them. He couldn't even trust the land line any longer. Meeker, or whoever was running Meeker, had those codes as well. The system, the network they worked for years to build, was falling apart.

He dropped his head into his hands. The files. Who had the files now? Martin might have found a way to protect them, but there was no telling how long it would be before he broke, if he was still alive. Had time already run out?

He stood and grabbed his bag. The plan had changed. He had to know if Martin was gone, and that still meant he needed to travel. He only hoped Martin's security had been equal to the task, that Martin had gone silent to avoid detection. It was a long shot, but it was the one ray of hope in the situation that Mason was unwilling to really push.

He didn't bother locking the door behind him.

***

The trip felt like it took forever. Martin's house, when he arrived, was still smoldering. Men in various uniforms picked through the rubble and talked quietly amongst themselves. A small crowd had gathered across the little suburban lane to watch the activity. Mason caught snatches of conversation, bits of gossip about the fire. A gas line rupture, someone said.

House went up like a fireball. The onlookers shook their heads and mumbled sadly about what a shame it all was. Such a nice man, another said. Horrible way to die.

Mason stayed just long enough to satisfy himself that Martin was not there. An ambulance came earlier and left with the body, he heard. A hospital name was mentioned. Mason got back in his rental and typed it into the GPS.

The hospital was twenty minutes away. He tried to steel his imagination as he drove, clinging to the hope Martin had survived. It seemed too fantastic Martin could have lived through what he had just seen, but Mason knew men to cheat death in many ways. Martin's house was just as heavily protected as Mason's own, if not more. Mason arrived at the hospital no more convinced of Martin's demise than he had been before he saw the burnt shell of that dwelling.

The automatic doors opened silently as he stepped toward them, leading him into a well appointed lobby filled with people, some standing in small groups, others sitting in marginally cushioned chairs arrayed against walls boasting paintings of pastoral scenes, flowery still lifes, and children playing in impressionistic landscapes. He walked up to a semicircular desk proclaiming itself as INFORMATION. Behind it, a woman dressed in drab uniform was scribbling on a pad while she spoke into the headset hanging from her left ear. She glanced up as he stepped before the desk.

"Be right with you," she promised, and went back to her call.

He bit back a response. The bureaucracy of hospitals was nearly as bad as the government. Paperwork, the last vestiges of the fading technology now known only to the largest of corporations and the most immense businesses, lay thick around her. It never ceased to amaze him how, as civilization became more advanced, the minutia of its operation became more instead of less pronounced. He suspected it was the fault of The Enemy, this compulsion to record even the tiniest detail of existence. At times like these he missed the simplicity of the past, before databases and spreadsheets, questionnaires and surveys, licenses and forms had taken the place of face-to-face meetings. People had become social security numbers, insurance policyholders, and telephone listings. He once again felt the weight of his age as the identities he assumed over the years flashed through his mind, with their individual birth and death certificates, registrations...

"May I help you?"

He snapped back to the present. "Yes, do you have a Harold Martin here? He would've come in just a few minutes ago."

"Just a moment, let me check," she said, turning to a computer terminal nearly hidden by the stacks of paperwork.

Mason fumed as the seconds ticked by. Most people have no concept of time, no idea how precious is every tick of the clock. Deep within the back of their minds they have only a tenuous connection to this world. They know their time is finite, that their final hour lies somewhere out there, near or far. They pretend it isn't there by ignoring the importance of the time given them. They sleep too long, play too long, find new ways to waste time, to kill time, though it is their own lives they are wasting, themselves they are killing. A while ago, Mason had come to believe everyone was born with a purpose and given just enough time needed to complete it. Some sensed they had gone so far afield of their purpose they would never accomplish it. They became The Enemy conscripts, desperately hoping to find reward in this world, no matter the cost. The Enemy never ran short of promises, never missed an opportunity to step into the self-deception of the disillusioned.

"Mr. Martin is in ICU with..." She stopped and looked up nervously. "Are you family?" she asked.

"No," Mason admitted. "A colleague."

She looked relieved. "I'm sorry, but only family are allowed to see Mr. Martin."

"I understand. Can you tell me what his prognosis is, at least?"

A moment went by while she considered her answer. The hesitation said much more than the actual words she uttered.

"I am sorry, but I can't release any information until the next of kin have been advised."

There seem to be no reason to remain. Mason thanked her for her time and left the hospital. He had mixed feelings about the news. Martin was alive, barely. How that would color events to come could not be predicted. For now, he let himself be content with the news of his friend's survival. Mulling on his future served no purpose than to distract Mason from what he had to do.

He needed to identify the Meeker impostor, defeat Azazel, and reinstall the North American cell. A tall order even if he had Martin and the others to help. As it was, he could trust none of them now. Not even Tripp, not since E-Yukon went down.

He needed a place to start, and that would be Martin's house.

***

"Oh, yeah. Definitely arson," the policeman told him. "Several people saw a black sedan leave just before the explosion."

"Anybody get a license number?" Mason asked.

"As a matter of fact, a witness said the tag was ANGEL. Strange, huh?"

"Yeah. Weird."

Mason left the policeman nursing the scratch on his hand. He needed to get to a computer terminal. A few minutes with that, and the backdoor program built into the DMV database by his cell more than ten years earlier would give him the name of the registered owner, although he could guess what he would find.

The GPS in the rental led him to a local copy shop advertising itself as an Internet café. The workstation was coffee stained and the keys gummy, but the connection was fast enough.

He wasn't surprised that the car was registered to an employee of Catalina. He was surprised at the name of the employee.

Michael Jenkins.

Mike.

Perhaps he had been overestimating Azazel's resources

after all. Whether he had destroyed Martin's house personally or sent somebody to do it for him, he'd used his own car. A few more minutes and a search of the local police report database explained that. Michael Jenkins had reported his car stolen the previous day.

Mason didn't know if Azazel had set this up as a backup plan, or as a double cross. Minions of The Enemy often acted chaotically, a reflection of their inner nature. There was no use trying to understand why they did what they did. He dealt with it and moved on. Trying to plumb the depths of their motives was a waste of time and resources.

He got an address in the database and plugged it into the rental's GPS.

It was time to take the battle to The Enemy.

7

Not surprisingly, the address was in the most prestigious part of the city. The neighborhood was heavily wooded estates of five, ten, and twenty acres with multimillion dollar homes nestled discreetly and securely away from the main road. Iron gates, in some cases flanked by a small security booth containing grim looking men, separated the tree-lined private drives from curious passersby. The place fairly reeked of money, power, and ambition. Exactly where you would expect to find Azazel.

He pulled up before the gate decorated with six trumpeting angels rendered in its wrought iron. Two very large men appeared behind it, dressed in dark uniform suits and sporting earpieces and handsets. One of the men peered at Mason, said something into his handset, and stepped aside as the gates opened. The other moved out of sight again behind the gates, as the first briskly waved him through.

So much for surprise, Mason thought, as he navigated the gate while keeping an eye on the guard. Azazel probably knew about their monitoring of the police computers and detected his investigation. Or it could be the guards had standing orders to let him through whenever he appeared.

In spite of himself, Mason was impressed with the estate's manor. Jenkins had replicated a German castle, circa 1300, down to the statuary on the lawn. Memories rose unbidden of the days of the Holy Roman Empire, memories he preferred not to recall but in which Azazel obviously reveled.

A man in a valet's uniform met him as he pulled up at the front door. Mason gave him the keys to the rental, which the man accepted with a wordless bow. The door opened in the front of the main house. A gray-haired man in formal wear appeared in the doorway.

"Mr. Mason," he said. "Mr. Jenkins is expecting you." He made a slight bow. "If you'll follow me, please." Without another word, he moved off into the house.

Mason stepped into an elaborately furnished foyer from which staircases rose on the left and right to an elevated walk circling the room. Straight ahead he could see a large great room dominated by an immense table around which were arrayed about twenty high-backed chairs. Guarding each bottom step of the stairs were life-sized statues of angels, trumpets held at the ready. The angelic motif dominated the room, in paintings, tapestries, and even the tiles in the foyer floor.

The butler ushered him to the right of the room, where double doors revealed a spacious parlor reminiscent of the rest of the house; dotted by angelic images in the divan, a pull string, the lamps and lampshades, paintings, and several half sized statues.

"If you will, please wait here. Mr. Jenkins will be right down," the butler invited.

Mason nodded and watched the man leave, unsurprised to hear the key turn in the lock. Obviously, Azazel did not want him wandering around unescorted on the grounds.

Since he wasn't going anywhere anytime soon, Mason decided to re-check his personal wards. Satisfied he was as safe as he could make himself and still be mobile, he turned to examining the room. It took a matter of seconds to discover the video and audio bugs. He left them alone. He had no intention of hiding his intent from Azazel. Still, he couldn't resist waving at the little video camera. They shouldn't assume he was a complete fool. Most people would consider walking into the enemy's lair less than intelligent. Azazel might not be convinced of that, but his lackeys could take it as a license for rash action. Best discourage that early on.

After an appropriate amount of time, which Mason concluded must have been for the benefit of Azazel's toadies, the Minion entered, grinning broadly. Two bodyguards, nearly identical to the men at the gate, flanked him.

"Jonah Mason!" Azazel gushed, sticking out his hand. "How the hell are you? It's been too long."

Mason crossed his arms. He knew better than to accept Azazel's hand. Unseen to the bodyguard, a heavy ward glowed on the man and the scent of lilacs was thick in that room. Azazel dropped his hand and laughed.

"Look, I know we've had our differences," the Minion said congenially. "Let's start over, shall we?" He waved off the bodyguard, who turned and left, closing the door behind them. "Better?"

"What happened to Meeker?" Mason said brusquely.

Azazel looked as if he would try to deny any knowledge of what Mason meant, then, the grin dropping only a notch, he shrugged.

"Such a lovely girl," Azazel said, walking to get a drink from the decanters set on a table by the divan. He took two glasses from the rack above it and poured two fingers of golden liquid into each. "Drink? 15-year-old Scotch. My favorite."

Mason shook his head.

"Suit yourself."

"Meeker?"

Azazel sighed theatrically. "I really don't understand. Why go on with this charade? You can't win. You've already lost. He lost long ago. Why can't you accept that?"

"Is Meeker still alive?"

"Why is that important?" Azazel said, sipping his whiskey. "She's just another woman."

Mason waited.

The Minion sighed again, this time in apparent exasperation. "Yes she's alive, if it means anything," Azazel said.

"Where is she?"

"How should I know? She's your operative."

"Where?"

They stood staring at each other for a few moments. Mason watched the man's face change from bored amusement to impatient annoyance. The pressure of silence weighed heavily on Azazel, he could tell. It was the one weapon The Enemy could not bear above all. In the silence was time for thought, time for contemplation of the future and the past. Time for realization of consequences.

"I spoke with Martin, you know," Azazel said slowly. "He's very stubborn." He sipped the Scotch, watching Mason for reaction. "An unreasonable man. I only wanted the files. I don't care about your silly resistance cell."

"Meeker."

Azazel snorted and tossed back the rest of the drink in a gulp. "I'll make you a deal. The files for Meeker."

So, Martin held out after all, Mason thought. What had he done with the files? Whatever it was, he'd done it so well Azazel had resorted to violence to try to force it from him, unsuccessfully.

"It's a fair deal," Azazel went on. "The files are of no use to you."

"I need to see Meeker before I agree to anything," Mason said.

Azazel's demeanor changed abruptly. Mason saw the Minion thought he had an angle.

"Of course," Azazel said, all congeniality again. "And I need to see the files."

Mason nodded. Let the man think he was in control. It bought yet more time.

"Very well," he said. "But the exchange must take place

at a time and place of my choosing."

Azazel shrugged. "No problem. Where and when?"

"I'll let you know."

"Don't make me wait," the Minion said, a dangerous edge creeping into his voice. "I don't like waiting, and I get cranky easily."

Mason walked to the door, stopping short at it to look meaningfully at Azazel. The man made a motion with his left hand. There was audible click for the door's lock. It swung open to reveal the butler waiting just outside.

"Expect my call tomorrow by noon," Mason told him, and followed the butler to the door without looking back.

***

Mason arrived back at his country home to find he had an unexpected visitor waiting.

The long black car sat in his drive, slightly off to the side as if to say it was willing to wait as long as necessary. The man leaning against it watched him pull past and into his garage without making a move from his station. He remained with the car even when Mason got out of his own vehicle.

Mason was troubled at this turn of events. Azrael's

warning came back to him now. Back then, he had considered Azrael's words a threat to one of The Army's cells. Now, he saw Azrael had meant something entirely different.

It would appear certain now that Azrael was above Azazel, and that Mason and his cell had fallen in with a minor officer. Azazel must have known of Azrael's earlier visit, yet he still came to Mason for help. Perhaps he thought Mason's involvement would somehow strengthen his own position. Perhaps Azazel was actually working with Azrael after all. Suspicious burst on him as he considered the black car's presence.

Was this all planned to compromise him and his cell in the eyes of the Master? They had been maneuvered into committing fraud and stealing files, ostensibly to protect themselves and The Army. Mason himself allowed this, knowing full well the consequences, balking only at the suggestion of turning over one of his own as hostage. The whole purpose of the dealing had been to save their cell from further damage. They had lost Chandler, Meeker, and Martin. Overguard was neutralized. And Tripp?

He frowned. Tripp? A sinking feeling grew. He hurried to the front door. Tripp had information about his house, knew about how the wards could be bypassed.

The front door was ajar.

8

Overguard considered Mason's order. While visiting the Italian cell, he could gather information on the research they were doing on a new weapon. The information might be useful to them in future, and actually seeing the prototypes would provide details critical to understanding its operation. On second thought, he remembered that the Roman cell was run by a man who had a reputation of being timid in confrontation with The Enemy. The Europeans had more on their minds than the protection of an expatriate American. With the worsening problems in the near East, they were facing a possible nuclear confrontation.

Overguard preferred not to get caught up in that. He had no illusions he might eventually have to, but for now he had his own problems, and it was possible the Roman cell might hold him there as a conscript, which they had the right to do. He couldn't afford for that to happen, and the thought of being separated from his own group worried him.

He suppressed a shudder. Was this Mexico all over again? The fiasco in Veracruz still haunted his dreams. The night sweats had stopped, but the memories would not leave him be.

He had been sent out to investigate suspicious activity near the coast, possible smuggling of arms to a local known agent of the Enemy. Any new supplies needed to be scouted and catalogued. It was critical in the volatile political theater of the failing Mexican government that they know of any new factors in The Enemy's favor.

Their cell didn't have the sophisticated resources Mason's had. Although they had access to the game, that would be useless in determining the exact threat. There was no more effective way of gathering the needed intel than to investigate personally. Someone had to go to Veracruz and, since he was fluent in Spanish and had been in Mexico the longest, he was elected. There was no reason to believe he would be gone more than a few days, and he would be in contact with the rest of the cell at all times through the subcutaneous communicators everyone in The Army used.

He left from Tampico early on a Thursday morning,

following the coast road in his Land Rover, but before he got as far as Tuxpan everything had gone wrong.

He realized now that The Enemy must have discovered his intentions. It was the only thing that made sense. Why else would that bus have crossed the line? Why else would it have forced him off the road and into the ditch, killing twelve in the process? He had been unhurt, but the bus overturned and burst into flames. The driver, wild-eyed, had stumbled from the wreck, blood streaming from a gash in his forehead, nearly incoherent, babbling about demons flying at his bus. The police assumed the man had been drinking. Overguard knew differently.

As soon as he could get free of the authorities, he tried, without success, to get in touch with the cell. He remembered the growing sense of dread as he patched up his Land Rover and hurried back to Tampico.

What he found there still haunted him.

That would never happen again. He didn't care what anyone, even Mason, said. He flew back to the States using newly acquired credentials as an American consultant to a British Petroleum firm, courtesy of his London contacts. His plan was to make his way back and reestablish contact with Mason in person. He wasn't sure what had gone wrong, but he wasn't about to abandon his people and go to ground. Martin and Meeker were off-line. Mason and Tripp were in trouble. Mason's order to run had shaken him deeply. The man was not one to give such an order lightly.

No one in the New York cell had any news, except to say the chatter was something big was going down in the Midwest. They would love to help, they told him, but without further details they couldn't spare the resources. It seemed the United Nations was meeting shortly to address the worsening European situation. The mystic problems would have to wait. To them, it was a "flyover country" intel dispute, a local skirmish. Hundreds of those occurred every year. The cells were created to handle such issues. If Overguard's cell were to fall, another would have to replace it.

They were expendable soldiers, after all.

Overguard got some concessions by hard campaigning. The security system the South Africans designed was put in place, giving them access again to the nationwide grid. It took several hours, but he located Martin in the hospital, his condition described as grave due to extensive burns and assorted other injuries. At least he was alive. He tracked Meeker to an Internet café outside Philadelphia, but there the trail went cold. Of Mason and Tripp he could find nothing. Whether that was good or bad, he refused to speculate.

He had no idea where Tripp actually lived, beyond it being somewhere in the Midwest. He did however, have a way of contacting Mason, an address outside Memphis he assumed was a safe house. As far as he knew, it was completely isolated, off the grid and known only to their cell. It was really all he had. He bought a ticket to Memphis.

***

Memphis International Airport was still overrun with cargo planes sporting the FedEx insignia. Since the collapse of the commercial airlines nearly forty years earlier, FedEx and the other major cargo haulers served double duty, at least for those who could afford it.

Overguard strode past the gate personnel without really noticing. He had his eye on the clock. Time was not on his side. Passing the closed registration desks, he noticed a young woman watching him, grinning. Something about her made him stop and look more closely.

"Janice?" he asked.

"Hello, Stephen," she replied.

"What the hell are you doing here?" he began, then

reached out to take her hands. "You look great. You colored your hair."

"And lost thirty pounds," she said, posing sideways. "You like?"

"Gorgeous," Overguard smiled. "But, why are you here in Memphis? You're supposed to be..."

"The same as you, probably," she interrupted. "Looking for Mason and Tripp." She pouted at him. "Why didn't you answer my calls?"

"Huh? I called you when I got to Berlin," he said.

Meeker shook her head firmly. "I got no calls from you. I thought you were reporting to Martin."

"But I spoke to you right after I got there," he insisted.

"It wasn't me," she insisted.

Overguard cursed. "When were you last logged on to E-Yukon?"

"What you mean?" she asked, genuinely puzzled. "We haven't used that for months."

He nearly shouted in frustration.

"What's going on, Stephen?" she asked in rising alarm. "I can't raise anyone on the land line and Martin's in the hospital."

"I'm not sure exactly," he said. "Can you tell me where you've been for the last few months?"

She passed a hand through her hair and sighed as she thought. "Well, I had a computer problem, so I ditched my lines and bought a new machine."

"How long were you offline?"

"Three days," she said. "Once I got back on, I logged into E-Yukon. Martin gave me some tips on how to better protect my new machine and Chandler sent me a root kit for..."

Overguard grabbed her shoulder a little more roughly than he intended. "Chandler did?"

Wincing, she gasped, "What's wrong?"

"Chandler sent you a root kit? Did you install it?"

"Of course. He said it was a new security packet from Central," she said.

"When was that?"

"Three months ago. Once it was installed, I swapped over to the E-Utah site. I know I'm supposed to have that next packet installed by now but..."

He let her go and grit his teeth. So, that was how it had been done. It wasn't her fault, he knew. She was too dependent on the rest of the cell for so much. He had brought her into The Army. Why had he done that, put her in that position?

"Stephen? Stephen, what's going on? Talk to me!"

He took a deep breath. There was one question he could

ask that would confirm what he suspected had happened. "When did you last talk to Chandler?"

"Yesterday. Why?"

He nodded. "Sorry, honey. Chandler's been dead for months."

She dropped her bags and covered her mouth in horror. "But that means..." Her eyes widened. "I didn't..."

Pulling her to him, he stroked her hair. "It's okay," he said. "We'll sort this out."

"Martin? Mason? Tripp? Are they...?" She choked on the words. "It's my fault."

"Stop that," he smiled at her. "We all were duped." He pecked her on the cheek.

"We have to get to Mason," Overguard told her, trying to draw her out of her funk. "I'm headed to a safe house."

"So am I," she said, a slight tremble still in her voice. "You think he's there?"

"I don't know, but, if he isn't, I'm hoping we can find something there to steer us toward it."

She picked up her bag. "Let's get going. My car should be here by now."

He followed her out.

***

The drive took them out of the city on an old divided highway, part of the aging interstate highway system. The medians were overgrown and rubbish was strewn heavily on the shoulders. The pavement itself was badly patched, with large cracks in the weathered concrete. Many of the access ramps were closed or blocked off. Traffic, such as it was, consisted mainly of trucks and paneled vans, with few private vehicles, probably locals. The little car rattled and lurched along at a maddeningly slow pace. Any other time he might enjoy the ride, with its picturesque view of the cattle farms and fields they passed. As it was, the bleakness of the landscape only served to aggravate his deepening anxiety.

What if this house outside Memphis wasn't Mason's at all? There were dozens of safe houses all over the country. Mason could have sought shelter in any of them, or none of them. He might be staying on the move to avoid detection. If that was the case, it could be weeks or months before they could re-connect. Overguard ground his teeth together and shook his head. He had to start somewhere, and from what little he knew about Mason, this place was the best bet.

He swung the car off the interstate and onto a two-lane

blacktop. The sun made its way toward the horizon as they drove deeper into wooded country, where rickety barbed wire fences separated the fields from the road. Dirt tracks broke off at odd intervals toward old farmhouses barely visible behind the thickening forest. Overguard nearly jumped when the GPS voice announced a turn in a half mile. He looked over at Meeker, who yawned widely and blinked sleepily at her surroundings.

"Where are we?" she asked.

"Damned if I know," he answered. "Podunk, I guess."

She made an amused sound and peered at the GPS map. "Are we getting close?"

"Gotta make a left here in a minute."

"Okay."

A little single lane led them off the main road into an oak forest. Overguard navigated the windy track at reduced speed in the dimming twilight, switching on the car's headlights. Mailboxes, most rusted from long exposure to the weather, hung on posts close to the pavement. Behind them the ground gave way almost immediately to a three foot deep ditch on both sides. Long-stemmed flowers and grasses rose from the depths to reach for the fading light.

The GPS informed them they were reaching their destination as they approached a white-graveled drive to their right. Overguard carefully guided the rental between the standing reflectors that warned of the sudden drop-off either side of the entrance to the driveway. The car rose briefly to crest a small hill and they passed through a set of open iron gates. The drive dipped downward just as the last of daylight failed.

The car reached the bottom. As the headlights angled upward, they saw the house, a two-story brick structure with a metal roof standing at the top of a rise with the wood pressing close on all sides. The hulking silhouette of a large black car was parked off the side of the drive, unlit by the warm yellow light that shone from the house's front windows.

Overguard stopped the car and peered suspiciously at the other vehicle. He wasn't sure whether it might belong to Mason, but he didn't want to take the chance he might be walking into a trap. The thought came to him again that this might not be Mason's house at all.

"Well," Meeker said. "Whoever they are, they know we're here."

She pointed at the doorway to the house. A figure stood there, lighting a cigar. Overguard watched the man for a moment. It was time to decide. Back up to the road and find another house? They would have to go through this again each time. Pull ahead, beside that black car, and get out?

The figure at the house left the doorway and walked down the drive toward them.

It was Mason. He looked just like his avatar. Martin had even captured the scars on the man's face.

Relief flooded through Overguard and he thought he heard Meeker sigh. He put the car in gear and crept forward to meet Mason. As he pulled alongside, he lowered his window. Mason leaned down and grinned at them.

"Welcome to Haven," he said.

* * *

Seeing Overguard and Meeker safe was a more than pleasant surprise to Mason. The fact that Overguard has disobeyed his order to go to Rome annoyed him, but he understood the man's need to find out what exactly was going on. Discovering that Azazel's story about Meeker was a tissue of lies should not have surprised him. Although it didn't change the fact their security had been compromised, it was comforting to know he could still count on his people to be loyal. Azazel had come very close to stripping them all of a key ingredient in being an effective unit: trust. Loss of that would have broken their cell just as effectively as killing them off one by one.

Mason walked alongside the rental car as Overguard drove it to a stop next to the black limo. His friends got out and he could see the concern on their faces as they glanced from him to the other car.

"Yes, I have company," he told them in answer to the unasked question. "And, no, it isn't Azazel."

"Then, who?" Overguard asked, slamming his door as Meeker rounded the rental's hood to stand beside them.

"Janice," Mason greeted her. "Nice to finally meet you."

Meeker smiled at him and put out her hand. "And you."

Mason took her hand and lightly shook it. "Have you seen Martin?" he asked her.

"Not yet. We heard he was laid up," Overguard replied. "That's about all. How is he? What happened?"

"Recovering. I'll fill you in later." Mason motioned them to follow and they fell in behind him. "Now, the wards are in place, just so you know," he warned them. "Standard precautions apply."

"Right"

"Okay."

"Our visitor," Mason said, "is Dorian Azrael."

"What?" Overguard blurted.

Mason turned to find them stopped at the bottom of the

porch stairs. Even in the yellow light spilling through the open door, they looked pale.

"Why is he here?" Overguard asked.

"Because we have something he wants."

Meeker spoke up. "The Catalina file?"

Mason shook his head. "A way to get to Azazel."

The others exchanged a puzzled look.

"Come inside and I'll explain," he invited.

After a moment's hesitation, Overguard and Meeker stepped through the doorway. Mason pulled the door shut and muttered a new ward over it. He signaled them to precede him into the main room, where Tripp sat watching Azrael lean against the fireplace, gazing into the flames that played along the gas logs. The Minion looked up as they entered, drawing himself to his full height and then bowing slightly as they approached.

"I believe no introductions are necessary," Azrael said. "Nor, indeed, would be wise," he concluded with a wry grin.

"We will be brief, as there is much to do and little time, as the saying goes," Mason stated. He looked at Azrael, who took the hint.

"Some time ago I came to... Mr. Mason here and asked him to abstain from becoming involved in events anticipated by me. Unfortunately, I did not foresee the extent of involvement to which you and your friends would be embroiled."

"Unwillingly," Overguard inserted.

Azrael nodded. "Understood. My subordinates are seldom so blatantly ambitious. I regret you have all been victims of this cockroach's plans." He paused to look at each of them in turn.

Mason tensed as the scent of lilac wafted subtly in the air. At the edge of his consciousness he could sense a darkening around them, a pall that left a dryness in the back of his throat. He frowned in alarm. The wards in the room hummed.

"I need a favor. I am sorry to have to ask *you* to do this," Azrael continued, in a tone that said he would rather have the pleasure himself.

"Oh, boy," Meeker mumbled.

"I understand your concern," Azrael went on. "I know my subordinate has done irreparable damage. I am also confident you are already taking steps to remedy that. Your cell security is nothing to me. The elimination of a threat to my authority, however, is. To that end, I want you to erase him and his cronies."

The scent of lilac flourished in Mason's awareness for a moment and he realized Azrael was holding himself in check with an effort. They glanced back and forth at each other, then Overguard and Meeker looked at Mason.

There it was again. The unspoken delegation of authority. The weight of his years lay heavy on him and the faces of those he'd led into battle over the centuries hovered just outside his mind's eye. He sighed and looked at the glowing ember at the end of his Montecristo. Once again, he stood at a decision point with no real choices to make. The events of the past few weeks had been one long series of predetermined results. He only hoped the Hand that had guided them this far had not been that of blind Fate.

He looked at Azrael. "We'll see what we can do."

9

Azrael had gone and the three were left alone to consider the turn of events.

"I don't like it," Overguard said for the fourth time.

Mason chucked the stub of his cigar into the fire and rubbed his fingers together to dislodge an errant tobacco flake.

"So you've said," Tripp pointed out from his place in the high-backed chair.

"Well, I *don't*," Overguard growled. "How did we end up working for The Enemy?"

Mason turned to them, leaning against the mantelpiece. "We're not."

Overguard looked at him sharply. "We're not? You mean, we're not going after Az— him?"

"Oh, we're going after him all right," Mason answered. "We're going after a Minion causing trouble. It's what we've always done."

"And how is that not working for the guy who just left?"

Mason sighed. "The Minions are constantly at each other's' throats, you know that. The fact that we know our goals coincide with that of an Enemy now makes no difference. Hasn't the possibility that we have been the unknowing tools of some Enemy plot in the past ever occurred to you?" Overguard's stunned reaction was his answer. Mason shook his head. "Whatever the reason on the surface might be given for us taking on our opponent, I have faith that *our* Master is using us to His advantage."

The others silently pondered his words, the soft hiss of the fireplace filling the void. Mason walked over and poured himself a whiskey. He wished he believed his own words as earnestly as he had spoken them.

"You're right, of course," Meeker said. "It's just that it's been so long since we operated anywhere but cyberspace..."

He nodded at her. "Yeah. Cyberwar is bloodless maneuvering. We've become separated from the reality of what The Enemy has done to this world. Maybe this is His way of bringing us back to Earth, as it were." He sipped his drink. "I believe what's happening here means the Conflict may be ramping up. We need to get out from behind our desks and back into the trenches. Things will be different, Janice. I'm sorry, but you are about to find out what it really means to be a soldier, and it isn't pretty. But it is necessary."

Overguard grunted his agreement. "You're probably right. It just galls me, is all."

"Soldier up, bud," Mason said with a smile. "I have a feeling there's worse to come." He poured another whiskey and handed it to Overguard. As the other man accepted the glass, Mason was hit by a sense of *deja vu*. How often in the past had he stood just so on the even of battle, sharing a moment with comrades who had never seen another sunset? Ten times? A hundred? He closed his eyes and pushed the feeling away with an effort. Another unpleasant side effect of a life spanning centuries: the repetition of past actions.

Yes, he thought, now is another of those times.

"So," Tripp said, bringing him back from his thoughts, "what's the plan?"

They looked at him again, but this time the weight of his years was not so heavy.

* * *

That night, they worked out the sleeping arrangements. Luckily, the house was big enough to accommodate them all in separate rooms and they were assigned their bunks accordingly. Overguard stood out on the front porch, watching the stars overhead. It had been a long time since he had been able to see them so clearly. He had forgotten how beautiful they were.

"Penny for your thoughts."

Meeker closed the front door behind her and came to stand beside him. He smiled at her and looked back at the sky.

"Just enjoying the view," he said. "You know, there was a time when this wasn't so uncommon. I didn't realize how much I missed it."

She was silent for a long time as they both watched the stars. A falling star streaked its way behind the trees. For some reason, he was reminded of the telephone conversation he had with her impostor, and the feelings it had caused sprung up. Before he realized it, he was speaking.

"I have to admit I was a little hurt when I talked to you in Berlin."

She frowned at him. "I already told you that wasn't me."

"I know that now."

He turned to look at her. A lump rose in his throat. It wasn't until right then that he realized how much he dreaded losing her. The conversation with her impostor had hurt, but this was agony. How do you confess to someone that you've betrayed a secret so personal? Could he do it? He could lie, tell her anything but the truth. He was sure she would accept it, but there would always be something between them, a guilt-ridden cloud that could never be dismissed.

"Janice, I..." He stopped again.

She must has sensed his unease. She put a hand on his forearm.

"Shhh," she said. "Stephen, it's okay. Whatever is bothering you, you can tell me."

Could he, really? Did he trust her feelings for him so much, he could risk them with this?

"What is it, love?" she asked. "Please, don't shut me out."

He felt like he wanted to explode. He covered her hand with his own, hoping to hang on to her as he fell into that abyss of fear that hovered nearby.

"Whoever was impersonating you didn't know about us," he managed to get out. "Not at first. I'm afraid... I'm afraid I let a little too much slip."

Her expression changed just a little, enough to frighten him, but not enough to stop him now that he had made the decision to reveal his actions. No matter the consequences, he had to tell her the truth. She deserved to know. Perhaps she would see that he had not meant to betray her trust. Perhaps she would understand why he had done it. He took a deep breath.

"I talked about Haltwhistle," he admitted. He felt the shock in her touch. "Please understand," he went on hastily, "I thought it was you, and you were so cold and distant. I was just..." He stopped as she pulled away and turned her back to him. "I was just hurt. I was trying to get through."

"Haltwhistle," she breathed.

He wished he could see her expression.

There was a hotel in Haltwhistle, a little town in Northumbria, England. The town touted itself as the center of the British isle and even sported a signpost with directional flags to various locations in Scotland and England. The hotel was across the street from the signpost, its front painted a yellow that reflected sunlight on to the little lane separating them. He and Janice had spent a week there, a week he treasured more than anything.

She had been a new recruit to The Army, and maybe it wasn't right what they had done. Maybe it wasn't ethical that a man of his age should become involved that way. But did he have any regrets? Did he feel guilty? No. For the first time in a very long time, he felt young again. In her arms, he breathed life anew. The decades dropped away and the memories of what happened in Mexico, the events that cost the lives of so many of his cell there, faded.

He had fled to Amsterdam to forget, had withdrawn for years from the Conflict, from everything. Then Central had approached him in his sanctuary. It had been a Knight, he was sure, that visited him in a dream. The vision instructed him to contact Mason as soon as possible, but he had balked. For weeks, he mulled his orders, knowing that the Master would not force him to comply.

It had been the bombing of the Vatican that convinced him. Even now, he was ashamed to admit it had taken an atrocity of that magnitude to convince him of his duty.

But he had forgotten even that as he shared that little bed in the Haltwhistle hotel. Janice had resurrected in him his will to go on. She had given him something to fight for besides his duty to the Master.

Was that a sign of how shallow he really was? That the affection of a woman was more to him than duty? He didn't know, and right now he didn't care. The only thing that mattered to him was her forgiveness, but did he even deserve it? They had kept that week a secret for so long. It was theirs alone, something only theirs, a precious memory between two lovers.

His heart leapt into his throat as she turned back to him, tears in her eyes. He almost gasped as she ran to him, embraced him, and their lips met.

"Oh, Stephen," she murmured. "I understand."

As they kissed again, he didn't hold back his own tears.

***

Meeker held him tightly. His confession at first confused and appalled her. Haltwhistle had been very special to her. She thought it had been special to them both. Stephen had been so gentle, so attentive. Had he just been playing her? She couldn't bring herself to believe that.

When she first met him, she had been on a trip to visit her cousin Ella in Amsterdam. She'd been there before, so she wasn't distracted by the canals and shops any more. Sure, the novelty of the ready availability of marijuana and sundry other less legal drugs was interesting, although she never indulged. And the city itself was an experience visually. Still, just like anywhere else, after a while it became just another place.

She and Ella walked into a little cafe for a quick snack.

She was partial to cakes and pastries and secretly made it a point to eat as many as possible while she was in the city. It was her one vice, sweets. She felt absolutely terrible afterward, but it was an exquisite guilt.

He was sitting in front of a cold cup of coffee, staring at nothing. He wasn't handsome, but he wasn't exactly plain either. There was just a touch of gray in his hair that spoke of some hard experience, and the pain in his eyes touched something in her. Her cousin noticed her interest and jabbed her in the ribs.

"Stop staring," Ella said.

"I'm not," she objected, turning back to her *stroopwafel*.

"You were, so." Ella looked at him again. "He *is* kinda cute. Maybe you should go talk to him."

"No!" Meeker snapped.

"Why not?" Ella grinned, obviously enjoying herself.

"Stop being a jerk."

Ella made a face at her, but relented. "Finish your pastry. We'll miss the movie."

He was still there when they left. He might as well have been made of stone for all he had moved. What could he have been thinking about?

The next day Ella was called back into work. Meeker

told herself she was going to the cafe because the *stroopwafel* there was so good, but when she arrived she was disappointed to see he wasn't there.

What had she expected? That he would still be there, staring into the air, twenty-four hours later? She took her coffee and sweet to the only empty table and settled in to chide herself for a fool. He hadn't been that good-looking anyway.

Her heart nearly stopped when he walked through the door. He was taller than she thought, better built. The pain was etched into his features, but his eyes, blue and clear, were alive and focused. She felt an energy coming off him she hadn't noticed the previous day. It seemed odd he could have been so morose yesterday. If she hadn't seen it, she wouldn't have believed his mood could have been so dark.

He walked up to order his coffee. It was then she realized there was only one empty seat in the cafe. The one across from her. She nearly choked on her pastry. How had that happened? For a moment, she considered getting up and leaving, but at that second he turned to look for a place to sit. Her heart thundered in her chest as his eye lit on the empty spot in front of her. She felt like running, but something held her, even when he approached her table. She felt mesmerized.

"May I?" he asked. His voice was a quiet baritone

rumble.

She managed a smile and nodded.

"Thanks." He slipped into the seat. "This place is really busy today."

"Yes, it is," she said.

He smiled at her. She liked that smile.

"Stephen," he said, offering her his hand.

"Janice," she said, taking it.

"Nice to meet you, Janice."

The days that followed were a whirlwind of memories now. She had never felt about anyone the way she did about him. Maybe she was hypnotized by his charisma, maybe she was caught up in the paradox of his laugh and the haunted look she often saw in his eyes. He had a way of looking at the world different from anyone else she knew. Slowly, he came to trust her to the point of openly discussing the existence of The Army and his place in it. Nevertheless, it was weeks before he told her what had really happened that sat so heavily on his spirit. The horrific events surrounding the end of his cell in Mexico and his move to Europe came out at first in hesitant phrases, then in more detail as they drew closer together. She learned of his pain and shared it with him, holding him as he finally allowed himself to grieve, and listening to him as he admitted his guilt of being a survivor.

Then, when at last they had come to be so close, they sneaked away for the weekend at Haltwhistle to consummate the relationship. It was then she realized that whatever he was, whatever he believed, was who she wanted to be and believe. And, standing there in his arms on Mason's front porch, she felt that more strongly than ever before.

***

The disturbance in the wards brought Mason to his front window. Meeker and Overguard were standing on the front porch, looking at the stars, and he was reminded of his unease about Overguard's recruitment of Meeker on his own.

Bringing people into The Army was not just asking them to join a team. It bound the recruit for life, and beyond. Certain abilities were given to the candidate by a higher authority upon acceptance into the ranks, abilities not immediately evident to any but the spiritual powers. By committing to The Army, the recruit became an instant target of invisible forces. Until they mastered their newfound abilities and were able to survive on their own, a veteran saw to their protection. Many were lost early in their career for leaving that protection too soon, whether by accident or design. That Overguard had not exercised his duty as Meeker's protection deeply disturbed Mason.

As he mulled what to do about Overguard's oversight, he saw them suddenly embrace. Instantly, he understood why Overguard had recruited her and his concern for Meeker's welfare dimmed. Whatever the man had done in the past, was done. There was no changing what had gone before. No one understood that better than Mason. What mattered from this moment forward was how they bound together for the events facing them.

Mason smiled and turned away. Let them have what time they could. Who knew what was to come?

***

Mason arrived at the hospital early the next morning to find that Martin had been moved into a private room. His burns, although serious, were responding well to treatment. Mason was not allowed to do anything but find out about his general condition, and that bothered him. The increasing bureaucracy in hospitals was a mixed blessing. Although it hindered access to patients by non-medical personnel, it wasn't a guarantee. And Martin was in no condition to protect himself.

The odds were that Martin might become a target again if they couldn't eliminate Azazel quickly. He wished there was a way to keep Martin out of this, but, short of having Overguard and Meeker guard him, there was no real way to do that. He left the hospital frowning in frustration. The staff wasn't very helpful when he asked how long Martin might be held for treatment. The uncertainty only added to the urgency of their situation.

Simply attacking Jenkins' manor was out of the question. Beside the fact it would take a small army to penetrate his security, it would bring undue attention to them and the Conflict. The attack would have to be both subtle and quick; a single, lethal blow. That meant they needed the kind of help they seldom asked for and were even more rarely granted. The Enemy and their Minions could operate openly in the world because their authority was derived from the world they made. Whenever The Army needed outside help, it had to appeal to a select group called Knights.

Knights were The Army elite. Their ranks were filled from those whose past deeds distinguished them in the eyes of the Master, and as such they were few but extremely powerful. They were dispatched to deal with the most significant needs, and only the Master had authority to do so. There was no procedure for requesting their help. No one knew who they were or where they stayed. Whenever they appeared, they appeared suddenly and without warning, but always and only in response to the most critical need. So it was that Mason was both elated and alarmed to find not one, but three Knights awaiting his return from the hospital.

Outwardly, they looked like anyone else, just two men and one woman lounging on his front porch. It wasn't until Mason pulled the car to a stop and got out to challenge them that he sensed the aura of raw power emanating from them. The trio approached, smiling, waves of strength and hope rippling almost visibly away from them.

"Septimus Vernus," the woman greeted him. "I am Jaelon. This is Antonius Malthusan and Krato Populus. We carry greetings from Him and are at your disposal."

Mason bowed for lack of knowing what else to do. He'd only fought beside Knights once before, during the conflict that came to be known as the Sixth Crusade, where he distinguished himself at the sieges of Jerusalem, Nazareth, and Bethlehem. Even though he had fought under the command of a man ejected from the Church for political reasons, he had been proud to work against The Enemy in that campaign. Seeing these Knights brought back memories long buried, good and bad. He shook them off as Overguard and Meeker emerged from the house. They looked as startled as he was to see the Knights.

"Are they... ?" Meeker began, a little breathlessly.

Jaelon looked at her. "We are His servants," she said. "Sworn eternally to Him."

Meeker smiled weakly. Mason understood her discomfort. Being with Knights was the kind of situation that made even people like himself, with more than a millennium of experience in the Conflict, feel small and awkward, little more than a child in the company of adults.

These were the beings who had seen the Face of the Master, had literally heard His Voice. They had none of the doubts or questions that sometimes plagued even the most veteran of Army troops. They *knew* the Cause was just, and that surety emanated from them in an air of confidence and determination that was contagious.

After the initial shock, Mason found himself warmed by their presence. There was a peace around them, a subtle component of surety of justice that, though not immediately apparent, sank in soon enough. In that peace, Mason found an immense solace as well, as though he had been reassured of his worth in the Master's eyes. The overall effect was a lifting of his spirits which he hadn't felt for a very long time.

"How may we help?" Jaelon asked.

Mason looked at the others, then turned to the Knights.

"We need a diversion," he said. "What we have to do should not be your responsibility."

Jaelon looked at him with eyes that nearly shone. Mason had all he could do not to turn away from that gaze.

"Our responsibility is not yours to define, Jonah Mason," she chided gently.

Mason felt confusion and the beginnings of shame rise unaccountably within him. "I meant no disrespect," he offered.

"Nor did I," Jaelon replied. "I merely wanted you to know that there is no need to feel you must protect us." She smiled again, her tone softening further as she went on. "Be assured, He knows your heart no matter your method."

Just as unaccountably, Mason felt comfort at that knowledge.

"Very well," he said. "Then, here's what we know.

"Azazel's house is a fortress surrounded by a high wall, undoubtedly warded, and protected by a troop of guards. Short of a full-scale military assault, we're not dislodging him from there. Luckily, we won't have to. We have some computer files he wants and he has demonstrated he is ready to do just about anything to get them. He has already met with me personally, so I am sure another meeting can be arranged."

"What exactly do you intend to do with him?" Jaelon interrupted.

Mason paused. He was reluctant to put it into words, but there seemed little choice.

"He must be stopped for the sake of my cell's safety and security," he said. "I intend to kill him if necessary."

Jaelon's expression went grim and the other Knights crossed their arms and scowled.

"So, they call you Angelkiller for a reason," Malthusan said.

Mason bristled at their air of disapproval. "You have a better idea?"

"You cannot kill Azazel," Jaelon stated flatly. "It is impossible to kill a Minion."

"I know that," Mason retorted. "But I can destroy his physical manifestation and send him back."

Jaelon shook her head. "Have you forgotten how The Enemy works?"

"They possess, inhabiting the body of a human," Populus put in. "Azazel must be ejected from the host, yes, but preferably in a way that does not kill the victim of the possession."

Mason inwardly cursed himself for his forgetfulness.

He leaned back against the car and grit his teeth.

"How long has it been since you directly fought a Minion?" Malthusan asked.

The question caught him off-guard. How long, indeed? Since before the turn of the 19th century? That long?

Jaelon put a consoling hand on his shoulder.

"Be at peace," she said. Her touch was warm and comforting. "You have carried this burden for many years. Let us help."

"Draw him out," Malthusan said. "We will do the rest."

"It is why we were sent," Populus told him. "Once the decision was made, even though the authority behind it was that of an Enemy, our path was opened."

"We can save Michael Jenkins, if he wants to be saved," Jaelon said. "Give us the chance."

Mason suddenly realized what they were saying. *He* was the impediment now. The Enemy had abandoned Azazel for its own reasons. There would be no help from that quarter for the Minion. What most concerned the Knights, and what should have been his concern, was the well-being of the person who had given over his life to The Enemy. This would be Michael Jenkins' second chance, something very few of The Enemy's servants were ever afforded. That was why the Knights had been sent. Not because of Mason's need to accomplish his mission, but for the sake of one human life.

He felt ashamed and humbled. He had been too long immersed in the everyday, mundane activities of an increasingly skeptical world. The poetry of life, the Light of spirit, was bleeding out of him daily, unnoticed. He had forgotten the reason he joined the Conflict: to fight against the Dark, to push The Enemy out of this world and back into the great Outer Darkness from which it came. Standing here, now, in the presence of these beings whose every move, every breath, was guided by that, helped him re-focus. His purpose was renewed. He felt alive once more, unhindered by age or doubt. He understood their concern for Jenkins better; the sanctity of life was not tempered by a bad decision made at a time of personal despair.

There was the difference between them and The Enemy. For them, life was precious, the Master's gift, a boon to be treasured and savored. To The Enemy, life was a tool to an end, the ultimate goal The Enemy used everything towards: to hold onto its power, to defy and deny the Master of Light and Life.

"Of course," he said. "Of course."

Jaelon's smile broadened. "Shall we go inside?"

* * *

Jaelon, who was once a Pictish warrior, had an intuitive sense of strategy and tactics. Mason was strangely comforted that she was about his age, chronologically. It gave him the impression he and she could communicate more as equals than he could with the other Knights.

Malthusan, a former Cypriot mercenary in the Crusades, was a fearsome fighter, fearless and strong. Physically, he was imposing, with a body builder's shape and a countenance that continually scowled. Mason felt he disapproved of this mission, but couldn't get Malthusan to speak to him readily.

Populus was an engineer whose grasp of structures and their weaknesses extended to machinery as well. He had made clockworks for an Arab Caliph. Smaller in stature than Malthusan, he had the lean look and swarthy complexion of the Mediterraneans. His eyes sparkled with intelligence and curiosity. Mason could see him analyzing his surroundings as he entered the house and was gratified to see the man nod to himself as he did.

Jaelon admitted that each of them had employed these abilities to great advantage during their earthly lives, but after their acceptance as Knights found that those talents so impressive in mundane conflicts were less than nothing in the greater Conflict. She was their spokesperson and talked with a gentle intensity that soothed and energized at once. By the time the plans were finalized, Mason and his friends had lost their awkwardness. The Knights had assimilated into the cell with the ease of a veteran company joining equals.

Populus revealed he had brought a large van. Mason assumed it was parked down the road, which was why they hadn't seen it before. Inside was all the amenities of a small apartment suitable for accommodating the three. Meeker said something about it resembling an artifact in a television series: bigger on the inside that out. Mason wasn't familiar with the reference, but he agreed with the description.

They weren't surprised to find sufficient armaments in the van to outfit a small platoon. What did surprise them was the type of weapons. Tasers, blinders, tear gas, concussion grenades, nothing lethal. After a moment's thought, they understood and never needed to ask.

The plan was simple. Mason called Azazel to meet at the park, where he would turn over the files in exchange for a binding oath of non-interference. The Minions might be duplicitous, but even they had certain rules they broke at their own peril. Once Azazel appeared, he would undoubtedly try to take the files by force, a double-cross. That would be when the Knights would strike. There remained a bit of uncertainty.

If Azazel stuck to the agreement, they could not move against him. Only deceit on the Minion's part could precipitate action. Such were the rules by which Mason and his troop were bound.

He was counting on Azazel to remain true to his nature. For once, he was actually hoping Azazel was lying.

10

"He seems genuinely concerned with the welfare of his people," Populus said.

The inside of the Knights' van served as their quarters while the rest of the cell bunked with Mason. None of the Army cell objected to their separation. In fact, Jaelon suspected they were relieved when she told them about it.

They were preparing for the confrontation with Azazel, a process not done by merely strapping on physical weapons. Direct conflict with a Minion occurred rarely, but when it did, it required special handling. Jaelon knew Knights were called upon only when necessary, only when the local Army cell could not be depended upon to cope with the situation. It was unlikely Mason knew that, and better he didn't.

Jaelon looked to each of her companions for input on whatever they thought might be of concern before facing

The Enemy, and, not unexpectedly, the subject of Mason had immediately surfaced.

"Let us not forget that he has struck deals with Enemy Minions," Malthusan said gruffly.

"We do not know the details of those deals," Jaelon pointed out.

"The details are immaterial to the fact that dealing with The Enemy is forbidden," Malthusan countered.

Jaelon huffed. "Vernus is older than all of us. He has been fighting in this Conflict all that time, and you think he has turned against the Master?"

Malthusan crossed his arms and glared at her. "Perhaps the years finally caught up with him."

"I disagree," Populus said. "The man is obviously loyal."

"Being loyal to the Cause does not make you immune to change," Malthusan stated. "We were sent to help this cell with their problem, but we all know that problem does not stop at Azazel."

Jaelon and Populus exchanged looks. Yes, they knew that, but how that related to Mason was uncertain. Malthusan was merely voicing what they all thought, but it still bothered her that he brought it up.

"We were not sent to prejudge," she told him. "We were

sent to observe. To assist. To support. Not to prejudge."

Malthusan lapsed into silence, but his eyes smoldered. Jaelon knew from past experience that he wasn't admitting defeat, just biding his time. She sincerely hoped that Vernus wasn't contemplating what Malthusan suspected.

"The rest of them surely would have suspected him if he had any plans..." Populus began.

"He is their shepherd," Jaelon said. She looked at Malthusan as she went on. "Much as I hate to allow it, it is possible he could be hiding something from them."

Populus grimaced at that.

"I am not saying that he is," she qualified, "just, that he could be." She shook her head. "When we rejoin them, you must remember our primary duty. We are here to help. Concentrate on that. There will be time for the rest later."

Populus nodded his agreement, but Malthusan's expression did not soften.

***

The sky was as clear and blue as he'd ever seen. The air, fresh with the aroma of blooming flowers, was warm and heavy with the promise of summer. Tripp breathed in deeply, savoring the essence of the earth borne on a sunlit breeze that quickened from the west.

"How is it?"

"Marvelous," he told the disembodied voice. "A beautiful New England day. I would swear I was back in Connecticut." He smiled and closed his eyes to better hear the chirping of robins and finches in the rustling trees.

Martin was a magician. He had taken Tripp's recollections of home and created a virtual reality so detailed is was hard to tell it from the real thing.

"Tripp!"

His eyes snapped open. That wasn't Martin's voice. That was...

Jaelon stepped into his line of sight. She crossed her arms and glared at him.

"What do you think you are doing?" she growled.

"Pardon?"

"Sleeping on duty?"

"What? No, I..."

"There can be only one punishment for such a dereliction," she said, lifting her hands. A violet glow grew between her fingers.

Tripp threw up his own hands to ward off the coming

blow.

And woke with a start, his heart pounding. Blearily, he wiped cold sweat from his brow. He looked around, finally remembering where he was. Overguard and Meeker grinned at him from their seats in the Knight's van, while the Knights themselves stood close to the door, talking quietly amongst themselves. He shuddered when Jaelon shot him a hard look, then turned and followed the Knights out of the van.

"Man," Tripp mumbled, "sometimes they give me the creeps."

"I know what you mean," Overguard agreed. "I think they even spook Mason."

"There *is* something about them," Meeker put in. "Like they're holding something back."

Tripp had to admit, he had felt the same thing. "I wonder," he said, voicing his doubts at last, "I wonder who really sent them? I mean, what do we really know about them?"

"Careful they don't hear you talking like that," Meeker said. "No matter who sent them, I doubt they'd take kindly to being questioned."

"Yeah. You saw how they shut down Mason when he talked about his plan," Overguard said.

The other two nodded.

"Do you think it's safe to leave Mason with them?" Meeker wondered.

Tripp shrugged. "Do we have a choice?"

They sat grimly considering that for a moment. Tripp looked at them, the two who had become one. They were what The Army was supposed to be about, the good in life. Love, companionship, the things The Enemy wanted bled out of humanity and, in spite of everything, couldn't.

Who was he? Just an old Yankee, been around a long time, trying to make the best of life when life kept trying to best him. He put on a good face, but where would it all go in the end? Would men like Mason, who had to go on and on for thousands of years fighting the same fight without end, be all that was left of humanity? Could they afford to lose such men?

"I'm going in," he said.

"What? No, we were told to stay put," Meeker objected.

"Mason's pulled my fat out of the fire plenty of times," Tripp said. He checked his weapon. "Cover for me."

"But..." Meeker began, but stopped when Overguard put a hand on her shoulder.

"Good luck," Overguard said. "Keep your head down."

Tripp gave him a quick salute, and headed out the door.

***

The park was emptying when Mason arrived. The rest of his company was already there, having set up a perimeter two hours in advance. Overguard, Meeker, and Tripp remained out of sight in the Knights' van on the north side of the park. Jaelon had taken position on the west, Malthusan to the east, and Populus south. Mason entered the park ten minutes before the arranged time to find Azazel sitting on a bench, watching people as they gathered themselves together to head home. He looked up as Mason approached.

"I've been sitting here wondering," he said without preamble. "You came alone? Or, did you?" He looked around. "No *visible* support. And yet, I find it hard to believe an Angelkiller would be so foolish. Call me paranoid," he laughed, "but you should know that I have taken steps to guarantee my safety and your cooperation."

"Is that so?" Mason said.

Azazel gave him a wry smile. "Your friend in the hospital has a visitor today. His... brother, I believe they said. Oh, wait, I didn't think Martin had a brother."

Mason was careful to keep his expression neutral. He gave a casual look around, noticing that they were now alone in the park. The light had faded to the gray of twilight and a fresh breeze quickened.

"Let's get this over with, shall we?" he said.

The Minion stood and brushed imaginary dust from his pants. "Let's. You have the files?"

Mason slowly reached into his pocket and produced a USB drive. "Your oath," he reminded.

Azazel grinned. "Ah, about that. I'm afraid there's been a change in plan." He shrugged in mock innocence. "Nothing personal, you understand. Just business."

"No oath, no deal."

The Minion laughed. "No shit? Now isn't that just too bad. I guess I'll have to take it off your dead body."

The breeze stilled. Mason sensed a growing heaviness in the air and the scent of lilac was suddenly thick as fog. He tucked the drive back into his pocket.

"You had your chance," he told Azazel.

"Funny," the Minion said, unsmiling. "I was about to say the same to you. You should have taken me out last time, Angelkiller." He raised his left hand.

"Azazel."

The Minion spun at the sound of his name to find himself facing Malthusan.

"What? Who are you? Angelkiller," Azazel chided, "have you been recruiting?"

"No. He's on special assignment."

Azazel shot him a puzzled look over his shoulder.

Malthusan uttered five words in a language Mason had not heard for centuries. The hair on the back of his neck stood up as the breeze quickened once more, carrying off the lilac scent and replacing it with the aroma of roses. The effect on Azazel was astounding. The Minion actually threw up his hands as if to ward off a physical blow and gasped. Malthusan spoke again and Azazel turned to Mason, raw hatred in his eyes.

"A Knight?" he choked out. He pointed an accusatory finger at Mason. "You've overstepped your bounds, Angelkiller, calling a Knight."

"It wasn't my decision," Mason shot back. "It seems your superior found you out. He has removed his protection."

Azazel went pale. "No!"

"Oh, yes, and without Azrael's protection, you must answer for your own actions."

Jaelon and Populus walked up beside him. Azazel looked nervously from one to the other.

"*Three* Knights?" he managed to strangle out. "Kind of overkill, don't you think?"

"That depends on you," Mason said. "You see, I have permission to send you back, but I'm not really fond of making anyone suffer needlessly. Even you. So, what about it?"

"You expect me to just roll over and give up?" Azazel said. "You have no idea what waits for me. The suffering. The pain. If I have to go back to that..."

"Your oath, Minion," Mason said. "You can stop this now by giving that oath."

Azazel spat at him. "That for your oath, Angelkiller! As if I would ever deal with the likes of you."

Jaelon muttered something and Mason heard a crackling begin, only it wasn't a physical sound. It was above that, beyond that. Azazel obviously sensed it as well.

Over the centuries, Mason had seen much. He had ridden with the Crusaders into the Holy Land, sailed around the Horn with Portuguese captains to visit India, trekked across the Gobi with a caravan transporting spices from Cathay, cut his way through the jungles of the Congo. He had seen men perform great feats of courage and cowardice. He had even once seen an authentic Cherub, a sight both inspiring and terrifying. He had never seen a Minion in its true form.

Until now.

Seeing Azazel's servants manifested had been annoying

and unsettling. This was far beyond that. Far beyond.

The twilight was naturally deepening, but another darkness settled over them as Mason stepped back involuntarily. The physical body of Michael Jenkins faded into that dark, enveloped by a growing wave of malevolence. Mason saw with an inner sense the silhouette of the Minion hovering over Jenkins. A low murmuring began from the Knights, tides of sound that broke against that shadow, sending ripples through it, drawing out of it a keening reply full of denial, pain, and defiance. The shadow swelled larger, twisting and turning formlessly as it did, thickening until Mason could no longer make out Jenkins within it.

A wail broke from the Minion, full of rage and hatred. Mason staggered under its impact, gasping for air. The sheer power of the cry drove him to his knees. He tried to shut it out, putting his hands over his ears, but the wailing wasn't merely audible. It echoed in his mind, clawing through his brain, a multi-legged thing scuttling with barbed feet through the tender flesh of his psyche. The pain was far worse than physical. It was a soul-searing agony, a burning brand on his most precious memories, a corruption leaving its taint on the recollections of centuries. He would never again remember anything of his life without recalling that pain. He howled back at the wailing, bringing from it waves of satisfaction and dark joy.

With the abruptness of a light switching on, another sound overrode the wailing. This sound carried hope and warmth, filling the ache left by that dark crying with calm.

Mason realized his eyes were closed. He vaguely remembered a deep pain, now scarred over and little more than a nearly forgotten idea, an impression of a possibility. He opened his eyes to find Jaelon standing between him and Azazel. She was his shield from the dark washing around them both, a shield remaining untouched by the flowing shadow, alive with Light from within.

As he watched, the Knights closed on Azazel, their constant murmuring an encircling ward that tightened with each passing second. Tendrils of light flickered around what was fast becoming just a column of black on black, nighted twilight, that swirled and twisted and folded into itself at the touch of those tendrils.

Mason struggled to his feet and shook his head to clear the fog of echoes of nearly forgotten pain. He tasted blood and found he'd bitten his lip, though he couldn't remember when. All his memories of pain merged, to slide beneath the layer of calm Jaelon broadcast.

The triangular formation had closed to within a few feet

of Azazel now. For all the cacophony in Mason's mind, the only physical sound uttered that might be heard by anyone else was the low rumbling from the Knights. Even that could be written off by the passerby as imagination or the sound of far off traffic. There was little to it that qualified as human speech. It was a vibration in the air, a quiet thunder. Mason knew it came from the three, but exactly how they were making that noise evaded him.

Silence abruptly accosted him, a silence so profound his ears protested against it, filling it with a loud hiss. It was the proverbial deafening silence, unnatural, almost painful in itself.

The darkness around them now held no further terror than a cold, starless, night. Mason heard the routine after-hours noises of a city park now: the rustling of the trees, a dog barking in the distance, the comforting background sounds of people going about their mundane tasks.

He peered around Jaelon. Azazel, or was it Jenkins? was on one knee, head down. Jaelon, Malthusan, and Populus stood around him, quietly waiting. The air was still thick with the aroma of roses. Jaelon spoke without turning.

"Send your friends to check on Martin," she said. "We believe he should be able to leave the hospital now."

Mason started to argue that. When last he had seen

Martin, the man had been months from being able to even walk. Then, he remembered who was speaking. He keyed the little communicator he carried in his pocket.

"They say go get Martin," he said into it.

There was a long pause.

"On the way," Meeker's voice came back. "You all right?"

"Fine," he replied, and closed the connection.

Azazel stood slowly, turning a full circuit to look at each Knight in turn. He stopped and looked at Mason.

"Why? We had a deal."

"Which you broke," Mason said.

Azazel shrugged. "You knew I would, didn't you? You've been dealing with us for, what? Twenty-three, twenty-four hundred years? Come on, have you ever known any of us to keep our word?"

"When it suited your best interest, yes," Mason countered.

"That hardly counts, does it?"

"The oath," Mason demanded.

Azazel crossed his arms, but remained silent.

"Last warning," Mason said.

"I'll take this one with me," Azazel threatened.

Jaelon raised her right hand and splayed her fingers wide. All three spoke a single word. A loud report thundered. Azazel crumpled to the ground.

"Wait," she said as Mason started forward.

Mason looked at her, puzzled. Usually, when a Minion left its host it was a fairly unspectacular event. The process of expulsion was initially violent as the Minion struggled to retain its hold. After that came a brief period of bargaining as the Minion looked for or tried to open a loophole to wriggle through. Finally, the Minion tried to kill its host in a last act of defiance. Beyond that, the Minion might manifest in a last ditch effort to terrorize its tormentors. It often momentarily broke through physically and, in a very few cases, actually injured the opponents. Mason wondered if Jaelon expected that to happen.

Quiet settled over them. The Knights stood patiently watching Azazel's recumbent form. Long minutes passed. The routine night noises wafted to them, this time including the growing noise of an approaching siren.

"Time's up, Azazel," Jaelon said. "You will vacate now."

Silence from Azazel. The siren became imperceptibly louder.

"Do you doubt we can call suffering on you even here?" Jaelon went on. "Then, know this."

Mason couldn't see what Jaelon did, exactly. From where he stood, her back blocked the view. He did, however, clearly hear her voice raised to a shout, followed by a heavy crack and a flash that momentarily blinded him. He blinked hard, trying to clear his vision.

"I will take this one with me, Knight!" Mason heard Azazel yell. "Leave me be!"

Another word, this time from Malthusan, followed by the crash, but Mason shielded his eyes.

"You will not!" Jaelon said. "You will vacate."

Azazel laughed. "Do your worst. Anything you do to me is nothing compared to what's waiting for me there."

"Then you leave us no choice," Jaelon replied. "Your host will die, Azazel, and there are none here to replace him."

"You're bluffing. That's murder."

"It is mercy."

"Your Master would never allow it!"

"The decision has already been made. Have you ever experienced death? It is an emptiness you cannot fathom. There is no pain, no joy. There is no sound, no sight. Death is a void, a non-existence. For those of us who believe in our Master, it is fleeting because he delivers us from it and takes us to His side. For such as you, there would be no such release. You would never be able to escape that void, imprisoned forever between this world and the next."

"You would condemn Jenkins to such a fate?" Azazel scoffed.

"No," Jaelon answered. "He will answer to my Master for his life and receive his just reward. He will not remain where you will be forever trapped."

"Death is preferable to..."

"One last thing," she interrupted. "One last thing for you to consider. In Death there is no identity. There are no second chances. Over eternity, you will slowly lose yourself to the void. Bit by bit, your very awareness will bleed away into that vacuum until there is nothing left that could be called Azazel. Eventually, the void will swallow you. You will pass from all existence and into oblivion."

Mason knew that was what every Minion truly feared. To be forgotten, to be denied. Just as they hated silence and had to fill it with whatever noise they could, they feared oblivion. Minions craved sensation above all else. They came from agony and pain and hatred to this world and wallowed in pleasure and greed and lust. To them, not feeling anything was the most feared of all punishment because they fed on emotions and senses. They used promises of wild satisfactions to catch a host and kept them by feeding off their desires. What Jaelon described was the antithesis of everything they craved.

"You're lying," Azazel said, uncertainty and fear creeping into his defiant tone. "How can you know? No one knows."

Jaelon shook her head. "No, Azazel, *your* kind does not know because you are what you are. Your Master has hidden many things from you, including the ultimate consequences of your actions."

Azazel laughed. "You talk like a fool."

"You have ruined lives and destroyed dreams," Jaelon went on as if Azazel had not spoken. "The time of your judgment is long overdue."

"And I suppose you think you can be my judge," Azazel scoffed.

"It is not our place to judge," Jaelon replied, "merely to deliver you for judgment." She signaled to the others. "You can at least save yourself the consequences of harming Jenkins by vacating now."

"Never! And you can't force me!"

"True. We cannot."

The Knights turned their heads to the sky as one. Azazel glanced nervously upward, then back to them. Mason couldn't help but do so as well. He saw only stars and an errant cloud. The park was still, even the breeze having paused. He noticed that the routine night sounds had also ceased, a silence that was unusual but not frightening, as when a roomful of people all stop speaking at once to catch a breath. The world, it seemed, was gathering itself to receive a thing of importance, the nature of which was significantly different to merit its undivided attention.

The darkness around them parted as a curtain, and from the rift shone a Light so pure, Mason found his heart in his throat at the sight. It poured over and around Azazel and the Knights, casting no shadows as it did. Azazel stood motionless, staring with wide, tearing eyes into that rift. His mouth worked but no sound emerged.

Mason felt a vibration deep within his soul, a chord of purest sound unheard with ear but stirring his heart to skip a beat. His gaze was drawn to the rift. The sound was coming from there, growing stronger. His legs began to wobble under the strength of that sound. It was a music not unlike a thousand trumpets sounding far off, or the movement of myriad feet along a surface made of crystal. His legs finally failed him and he fell to his knees. With an effort, he looked away from the rift toward where Azazel also knelt, eyes wider than Mason would have though possible. The Knights stood immobile, heads still tilted upward. Their forms shimmered, the Light passing through them as if they were smoke.

Azazel cried out and threw himself forward to lie completely prone, face down. Mason heard him sobbing and, for an instant, actually felt pity. From Mason's viewpoint he could see only light coming out of the rift. Azazel had seen into that vision, past the barrier between worlds and into the Presence.

Judgment, Mason now saw, was not something imposed, but something accepted. It was the awareness of one's failings and strengths. It was the knowledge beyond doubt of the finality of action, the certainty of consequence. It was the clear sight and understanding of one's role in all of one's life, the discovery of the deception that you are your own master, that you make your own destiny. It is the revelation of your fate, your reward, what you merit as justice when weighed against Truth.

That was what Azazel had come face to face with, and it had reduced him to despair. At least, so it appeared.

The Knights were again looking at the Minion. There was silence once more, though the rift remained open and the light still swarmed over them. Mason felt strength returning to his legs as Azazel stood to face Jaelon.

"What's going on?" he asked, looking around. "Where am I? Who are you people?"

There was no answer from Jaelon or the others. Azazel looked at Mason. The expression on his face was confusion and growing fear.

"Where am I?" he asked Mason. "What's going on?" He started to walk toward Mason. Jaelon stepped in front of him. He stopped, looking at her, puzzled.

"You must vacate. Now," she said.

"What? What are you talking about?"

Jaelon's hand came up and across the space between them. Azazel was lifted bodily and thrown several feet backward. He crashed at Malthusan's feet, crying out in shock and pain.

"Vacate," Malthusan commanded.

"Huh?" Azazel said, blearily.

Mason watched with a growing unease. The Knights' actions no longer seemed as called for, now that their target offered no resistance. He started to step forward, an objection forming on his tongue.

"Vacate, deceiver!" Malthusan repeated.

"I don't..." Mason began.

"You have been judged," Malthusan said, ignoring Mason's interruption. "Jenkins has been removed. You cannot remain. Choose, now. Vacate or face oblivion."

Mason choked back his words and blushed heavily. How could he have fallen for such a transparent ploy? What had become of his ability to discern The Enemy's deceits?

Azazel struggled to his feet. "Look, I have no idea what you're talking about. You're making a mistake."

Malthusan barked a word. Azazel staggered as if he had been physically struck.

"Why?" Azazel gasped. "What possible difference could it make to you that I should stay?"

"You have been judged. Vacate."

"This is murder! You can't possibly..."

"It is justice," Populus spoke up. "This you know. In spite of everything, we have tried to spare you oblivion. You have been given every chance."

Azazel laughed bitterly. "Is that right? Some choice! Oblivion or eternal pain."

"You made a choice long ago," Jaelon reminded him. "Now you must face the consequences."

"Look, maybe we can make a deal," Azazel began.

The light flickered, bringing Mason's attention back to

the rift. There was something emerging from it.

"You have made your final choice, deceiver," Malthusan said.

Mason gasped. A wave of an indescribable emotion swept over him, something like fear but heavily thrilled with joy. The noise coming from the rift swelled to fill his consciousness and everything around him dimmed as a being of intense Light swept into their world.

It was beautiful beyond words and terrifying beyond description at once. Mason could not tear himself away from the sight. So much of the being remained beyond that he knew he only saw the tiniest portion, yet what he did see took his breath away.

"Seraph!" Azazel shrieked in fear.

It was light and color, flowing from the rift and spreading around not just Azazel but all of them. Mason felt the raw power permeate his body, flood his mind and fill his soul. Somewhere far off, he could hear Azazel screaming, but that held no interest at all. He was totally enraptured by the warmth of the Seraph's presence. Its peace was that of the Knights magnified a million fold. No troubles could penetrate it, no tragedy darken it. The very fabric of reality, with its violent energy and roiling constant change, faded into nothingness. What remained for Mason was a vision of eternal fulfillment and certainty. His soul drank that in, for the first time realizing how parched it had been. His spirit sang with unfettered joy at a remembrance long thought lost. His lifetime of war and strife passed before his mind's eye. He wept at the stupidity of his doubts as the scope and goal of the Conflict was finally revealed. His fear that his involvement with Azrael would compromise him faded. His concern over the fate of his cell disappeared. At last he understood. He *knew*. Gone were all his doubts about the Conflict, his questions about the cause. The Knights might have seen the Face of the Master, but their confidence could be no more strong than his own now. He felt tears streaming down his cheeks unashamedly as his own actions over the years were justified at last. A great weight lifted from his soul and he wanted to cry out with that relief. In His own, ineffable way, the Master was giving Mason what he most needed now: reassurance.

The Seraph pulled back into the rift, but the effects of its coming remained. Jenkins' body lay lifeless on the ground, bereft of both the Minion they fought and the soul who played host to The Enemy. Mason didn't know the fate that had taken Jenkins, but he knew it was deserved. As to Azazel, there was no doubt in Mason's mind what had happened to him. As the rift closed and the sounds of the night returned, he marveled he had every felt pity for the Minion. He caught his breath and found himself smiling widely. He turned to Jaelon to share that feeling, but found her staring at him grimly.

"Now, Septimus Vernus," Jaelon said. "You have a decision to make."

Mason was stunned speechless. The Knights took up positions around him just as they had around Azazel.

"I don't understand," he managed.

"You dealt with The Enemy as equals," Jaelon accused. "You worked with them and furthered their plans."

"To protect my people," he countered. "It was necessary."

Jaelon shook her head sadly. "Where has your faith gone? Did you believe The Enemy so strong it could take from you that which you promised to Him?"

"No! Of course not!"

"Then, why? Why did you endanger yourself and your friends by consorting with The Enemy?"

"To save their lives," Mason replied, but he began to understand her even as he uttered the words.

"Their lives are not yours to save or give, Septimus Vernus," she said.

"You know what I mean," he said peevishly.

"But do you know what I mean?" she responded.

He took a breath, then nodded. "Yes. I do." And he did. She was making him say out loud what he had felt just a few short moments ago. It had to be said, had to be testified to them so that they would know he, too, had felt it.

"Then, here is your decision: what do you want to do? Remain here with them, possibly placing them time and again in jeopardy? You were forgiven once. Judgment may not always go in your favor. Do you trust yourself to make the right decisions every time?"

"No man is perfect," he admitted.

"Indeed."

In spite of everything, his concern for the others rose. To him, they were just children, caught up in a Conflict not of their design. Didn't he still have a responsibility to them? If he were to walk away from them, what would happen? Could they make it on their own, as much as they had come to depend on him? "But what is my alternative?" he asked, as much to himself as to Jaelon.

"To allow them to grow. They have come to depend overmuch on you. They need to learn to decide for themselves the best course of action."

"A cell needs a leader," he protested. "Without a leader, it becomes ineffective, uncoordinated, a danger to itself and possibly others."

Malthusan stepped forward. He loomed over Mason, his face set hard. "The time is past for such," he said. "The Master has decreed that a new era in the Conflict has begun, one in which individuals must fend for themselves. The world has changed, Vernus. It has become smaller. What once was impossible for a single person is now possible. Entire governments are vulnerable to attacks by lone warriors through media and computers. Most of the world is tied together by an electronic web, a web that can be used to accomplish what armies could not. But anonymity is key to success now, just as you had begun to realize. The Conflict has always been covert. It must now take on an even more invisible nature to continue."

"Your use of games was merely a test," Populus put in. "It showed the strengths and weaknesses of the new battlefield. Your cell and others like it were pioneers, ground breakers. What you learned and how you handled the dangers involved gave us critical information."

"That you reacted as you did when your cell was compromised showed a weakness in the system," Jaelon concluded. "Chandler did not cooperate with Azazel. His reward was death, but do not be concerned for him."

Mason hung his head. He felt sorrow at his friend's

passing, but relief at the Knight's words.

"The Master understands your heart," she went on, "and why you struck a bargain. The time for such vulnerability is past. The end of the Conflict is closer than ever before."

Mason's heart leapt at that revelation.

"We Knights have been but few until now," Jaelon said. "The cells have been rare and far between. That is about to change."

"How?" Mason had to ask.

"The time is soon," Populus said. "Knights are being gathered. More are being recruited."

"You can remain as you are," Malthusan said, "remain what they call an Angelkiller. Or you can become something more demanding. You will face greater dangers, more dire than Minions. The Enemy senses the end as well and he is mustering his own elite."

"There is to be another Great Battle, Septimus Vernus," Jaelon said. "It must be your choice as to what part you wish to play."

That was when the police finally arrived.

**

Tripp staggered to a nearby bench and collapsed full length on to it, gasping for air.

He had worked his way into the park until he could get a good view of Mason and the others. The confrontation between Azazel and the Knights had been impressive itself, but then had come the light.

He hadn't been able to figure out exactly what the others saw in that light at first. He could see Azazel's reaction, and that had been confusing until the Minion shouted.

What had he seen then? What was it that came out of that light? He'd seen some strange things in his life, but nothing came close to that. He still shivered to think about it, even though the memory was fading like a barely remembered dream. Had he really felt an indescribable joy, a flood of thrilling happiness on a baser feeling of peace and well-being that took his breath away?

He had been brought up a Puritan. His childhood had been a long series of sermons and strict adherence to religious ceremony. Over the centuries, he had followed Mason through some very disturbing situations, but he had never really considered anything associated with them as spiritual. Had he missed the point? Had he over the years forgotten the purpose of their existence, and Who was responsible for it?

There was one thing of which he was totally certain. He must see it again. Somehow, there had to be a way to summon it back, to bathe once again in its presence, to once more experience that soul-deep peace.

There had to be a way.

***

When they arrived at the hospital they had to navigate around a maze of police cruisers, fire engines, and ambulances. It was obvious something serious was happening, but no one paid attention to their van as they drove to the far end of the lot and parked. Overguard and Meeker strode through the main doors with a very short delay as a policeman checked their identification. Passing the guard, they found the hospital in an uproar. No one else gave them a second look as they made their way to Martin's room.

He was still connected up to a variety of tubes and wires, but he was sitting up and waved as they came in.

"About time you got here," he grinned. "You missed all the fun."

"Hello to you, too," Overguard snorted.

"What happened?" Meeker asked.

"Not sure," came the reply. "I think somebody tried to blow up the hospital." He pointed to a pitcher of water on a nearby table. "Do you mind? All this excitement is making me thirsty."

11

Mason sat in front of his computer and fingered the I/O port in thought.

The choice had been given, but how much of a choice was it, really? The Knights had actually given him an ultimatum: do penance or suffer the consequences. Not that he objected to the kind of penance they offered. In his younger days he might have been annoyed to the point of rebellion, but having seen what he had in all his years, he knew that would be the worst decision possible.

Jaelon had let him know that there was only one way to prove his decision. Dorian Azrael, with whom he had made the deal, had to be taken down.

In the case of Azazel, the protection normally afforded a Minion had been removed. He was vulnerable because of his superior's displeasure. Without the threat or guarantee of retribution, the Minion was on its own. It could not call on higher authority, since no authority above its immediate superior cared whether it lived, died, or went into exile. Each Minion served at the consent of its immediate superior, rose and fell in that esteem. Azazel had forgotten that, and had paid the price.

Dorian Azrael was another story altogether.

The Army had no information on to whom Azrael reported. To all appearances, he was the highest authority in his arena. Mason knew this was impossible, since it was well established that Azrael was a Minion, not one of the greater forces in the Dark Master's regime. It was possible that Azrael stood so high in the earthly hierarchy that he touched the lower rungs of that infernal ladder. If that was the case, and the more Mason investigated the more convinced he became it was so, then this would be the most difficult assignment he had ever faced.

He needed to work a way inside Azrael's armor and all he had that might work was the file folder Azazel wanted.

What didn't make sense was that the files in that folder were just routine invoices and a couple of pictures. Martin had run every decryption procedure known on them without finding anything out of the ordinary. How they could be used against Azrael boggled him.

The USB drive lay beside his keyboard, a little one-and-a-half inch rectangle. A Minion of The Enemy had bet everything and lost because of what was on that little fragment of technology. An entire corporate structure was thrown into disarray for the contents of that 12GB drive.

Contents?

He picked up the drive and turned it over in his hand. He looked from it to the I/O set. Why did Azrael pick him to get the files? Why him and not someone else? Azrael's corporation was global. Azazel had all the cells on the planet to choose from. Why pick his?

Unless, with the natural cunning of a Minion, Azazel had worked out a plan that required infiltration and control of an Army cell and his had been the winner of some random lottery. It wasn't as unlikely as it might seem that his cell had been picked by chance. The cell had been operating for more than a century. The law of averages said it would eventually fall victim to something similar. But, how could he use this to his advantage, turn it around?

Azazel hacked E-Yukon. Could there be something there?

He pushed the drive into the computer and booted the

game. As the program cycled up, he slipped the I/O around his neck and settled into his chair, flexing his fingers. The login screen appeared and he started to enter his password, but paused when he realized there was already a username and password entered, waiting for him to hit the submit button. "Dazzler" sat in the username window and the six black dots constituting the privacy shield for a memorized password blinked at him. They could only have come from the drive, although how Martin could have missed the data that forced that information onto his computer puzzled him.

He punched the Enter key, ready to quickly pull the I/O set off if needed.

A character selection screen appeared, with six characters displayed. He wasn't surprised to see avatars for Chandler, Meeker, Martin and the old dog. He was surprised to see one for himself and another that had to represent Azazel himself.

Mason couldn't resist selecting the Azazel avatar. The screen went blank and sounds he had never heard from the game before clacked, reflections of the visual, bewildering and choatic flashes on the screen. He struggled with the patterns for a bit, trying to make some sense of them, but after a few moments had to give up. Whatever it was, it wasn't a typical game avatar interface. He had stumbled on to something far more complex and, he suspected, the secret Azazel had been so keen to acquire.

He wished Martin was there, but, although the Knights had managed to remove him from danger at the hospital, a trick they had yet to explain, he was still too weak to move from the bed in the sanctuary chosen.

Mason logged on the old dog avatar out of curiosity, only to find the avatar blocked from usage by a blank screen announcing the character was no longer available for play and apologizing for the inconvenience. The other avatars had no such restrictions. He was alarmed at how easily he could access E-Yukon, considering the fact his personal account was locked out. Even more disturbing was the avatars for Chandler, Meeker, Overguard, and Tripp remained visible even though they were supposed to be offline. Above each hung a red dot, which he assumed meant they were inactive. He also assumed the dot changed color if the user logged on, giving Azazel cues as to who could provide real-time information. Whoever Azazel had hired to hack the game did an incredible job.

But surely Azazel already had access to this. Why did he need the files on the drive? The cell obviously had been compromised long before Azazel approached him. Chandler's death had been the result, not the cause, of the leak. There had to be some other reason Azazel wanted the files, and it probably had to do with that Azazel avatar.

It was critical he get someone to look at that, someone who had at least as much computer experience as Martin. The London cell had provided Overguard with a secure identity for his Berlin trip. They might have someone. He started to log off and reach for the secure land line, then remembered that, with Azazel gone, the game could be secure once more. Azrael didn't consider them a threat, and he might be right. Even with Azazel's files, they might not be able to get to him. Mason hoped this was one of those instances where the overconfidence of the Minion was the one weakness they could exploit.

Still, just to be sure, he could encrypt a message to Overguard in game as a test. If Azrael acted on it, he would shut down the game grid for good. He found the mailbox and typed in

I have 600 miles to go. Genius, eh? Oh, BTW, need 35g for maint of house

After checking the message twice, he hit SEND. The mail tablet vanished with a little "ding" and the virtual flag appeared. He picked up the land line and dialed Overguard.

"Go," Overguard answered.

"E-Yukon mail. Recon only."

"Got it."

They hung up. Mason pulled the I/O set off as he closed the game and removed the drive. The message, as innocuous as it sounded, was code for a meeting at a local restaurant late the following night. The restaurant was warded against any intrusion such that the owner, an Army operative, would know. If they were still compromised, then Azrael would send an agent to investigate, and considering he had personally approached Mason twice, the spy would be more than likely not just a human lackey. Still, it would be wise to take some extra, more mundane, precautions.

***

They arrived near the restaurant three hours before the appointed time and set up the wards in a two block perimeter. The idea was to catch anything that slipped past the restaurant wards, which might have been discovered when the game security was broken. Overguard and Meeker would remain in the Knights' vehicle which Mason and the Knights entered the restaurant.

They found the owner, Charles Trenton, talking to the cashier. Trenton clapped Mason on the shoulder.

"Mason! How the hell are you?"

"Not bad," Mason replied, wincing at the sting. "And you?'

"Can't complain. Well, I could, but what good would it do, ya know?" Trenton laughed. "What brings you to my part of town?"

"I need a favor."

"Sure thing. What's up?"

Jaelon stepped up, and Trenton immediately fell silent. He stared at her with an expression halfway between confusion and nervousness.

"This is Jaelon," Mason said.

"Um... Hello," Trenton managed. He looked at Mason, the obvious question in his eyes.

"She is," Mason confirmed.

Trenton's eyes widened. "What the... um... heck is going on?"

"Let's just say, the less you know right now the better," Mason answered.

"Yeah, well, what do you need?" Trenton asked with a sideways glance at Jaelon.

"There may be some unexpected guests here tonight. You have the standard wards up?"

"Always."

"If they pop, don't set off the alarm. Call me or her."

"You got it. Anything else?"

Mason grinned. "How about some of that killer eggplant parmesan?"

***

The appointed time came and went uneventfully. Although that was not a guarantee the game grid was secure, it was the closest they would come to knowing. The South African group hadn't yet finished their new code and, without Martin, Mason didn't feel comfortable experimenting with anything else. If they were going to move any time soon, if they were going to respond to the increasing world-wide tension reflecting the growing menace elsewhere, they needed to use those tools at hand, no matter the danger.

And the first step was decrypting the USB file folder. He needed Martin, and said as much to Jaelon. Martin was at his front door the next day, smiling from his wheelchair.

"How... ?" Mason started, then held up as Malthusan

appeared. "Oh."

"You have some powerful new friends," Martin said, chuckling. "Going to let me in?"

Mason undid the wards and stepped back as Malthusan pushed Martin across the threshold.

***

"It's some kind of data stream," Martin determined as he sat at the computer, the Azrael folder plugged in. "Not sure what kind, though. I believe it could be..." He blinked and shook his head. "Hello. There's something here." He sat quietly for a few moments, the I/O set around his neck blinking furiously, his expression one of growing amazement. He pulled the set off and handed it to Mason. "You better see this."

Mason took the set and slipped it on. There was a momentary disorientation, then he gasped as a landscape opened around him.

"The data stream seems to be a load for that," he heard Martin's voice from somewhere nearby. "I don't think it's ours."

Mason looked around carefully. Nothing about this VR construct looked familiar. The land around him was little more than desert lit by the ruddy beams of a dying sun. the environment was crudely designed, more for utility than entertainment. Three symbols appeared in the air before him. In alarm, he recognized them as angelic script he'd not encountered for centuries, three names.

"Pen. Paper," he said urgently. After a moment, he felt them pushed into his hands. Quickly, he copied the symbols on to the paper. Far off, he heard the rumble of Malthusan's voice, though he couldn't make out the words.

"Mason!" That was Martin, barely discernible. He heard the edge on that word and reached for the I/O set.

It wasn't there.

He clutched at his throat in rising alarm. What was happening? Of course the I/O was invisible in VR, but he was not actually present in that desert landscape. He was still seated at his computer, interfacing through the I/O.

Wasn't he?

Was it possible the improved immersion technology combined with this strange coding had produced an unexpected result? There was something more to this program, that was for sure, and the human brain was the template for computers, after all. Had the coding done something to him physically? Was that even possible? What if the coding had communicated to his brain the key to a new perception, reprogramming *him*, as it were, to a different plane?

Did that equate to a new plane of existence? Wasn't perception really how existence was defined? To a microbe, the world was a single drop of water, its existence mere survival. To a star, its existence would span light days or years of space. The human definition of existence was limited by the five senses and augmented, in a limited manner, by what ability the individual might have to interpolate beyond that.

Could it be that Azrael's company had discovered a way to open human perception to another plane? It certainly seemed to Mason that he was no longer in contact with the outside world, and this world continued to become more detailed as the seconds ticked by, as if the program was still loading. Vegetation appeared in the desert, familiar yet slightly odd, as if the programmer's concept of reality was altered by drugs or a different set of internal references. Things that shouldn't be threatening in appearance like flowers, grasses, and trees, took on a more menacing mien. The sky darkened into twilight against which the symbols burned starkly yellow, white, and crimson.

Each symbol now showed itself to be the first in a column leading hundreds of others, which stretched off into the distance behind them.

He forced himself to concentrate on those columns, drive down the rising anxiety that threatened to cloud his judgment. Obviously, the key into and out of this predicament lay in those symbols. Luckily, of all his cell, perhaps of the entire Army, he was the only one who actually could read it. The script had not been used for centuries by any Minion, most certainly the reason it had been used in this simulation. It was possible a Minion had mastered the intricacies of computer code and done this, but it was more likely the symbols had meant nothing to the lackey contracted to program them.

The primary symbols were plain enough. They were "Azrael," "Azazel," and "Andreal." Mason wasn't familiar with the last name at all, which disturbed him. Not that he considered himself an authority on The Enemy's hierarchy, but never to have seen a name so evidently important bothered him. Of course, it could just be someone one step down from Azazel, an even more minor functionary. In that case, was this Andreal a partner with Azazel in his rebellion, or just another pawn in the plan?

He raised his hand and touched the Azazel symbol. It shifted upward to tower above three other symbols, also angelic script. He tapped one and it, too, rose to hover over three symbols.

It was a chart, a blueprint for Azazel's organization! Was it possible the chart included Azrael's structure as well?

Hesitantly, he touched the Azrael symbol. It rose to stand over five other symbols, none of which were Azazel. Mason frowned. Had he been wrong about Azazel being Azrael's subordinate? He looked again at the Andreal symbol. When he touched it, two symbols appeared below it, one of which was Azazel.

So, Azrael had allowed them to think Azazel was the subordinate who had plotted against him, when Azazel had merely been working for this Andrael. That had to mean...

He checked the script below Azrael's name more closely and found Andreal was one of the five displayed.

The situation was a bit more complex than they thought. If they succeeded in unseating Azrael, they merely accomplished what Andrael had intended all along. It was blind luck they still had the USB file. It was even luckier it had been him and not Martin caught in the interface.

Mason paused. Luck? He knew better. In the Conflict there were no lucky breaks, no coincidences. He grinned at the complexity of events that led to this moment. All the ways it could have gone wrong. All the thing that looked to have been beyond their control. None of which had even been beyond His.

He turned his attention again to escape. None of this information would do them any good unless it could be extracted from the VR. There had to be a way out, short of complete shutdown, which might corrupt the files.

An idea occurred to him, so simple he wondered why it hadn't come to him before. Mentally holding his breath, he envisioned the I/O port around his neck and reached for it. His fingers found the set. Closing his eyes to mitigate the inevitable disorientation, he pulled it off.

He was back in his office with Martin and Malthusan. The men looked at him with concern.

"Are you all right? You're white as a ghost," Martin said.

"How long was I under?"

The others exchanged puzzled looks.

"What do you mean?" Martin wanted to know.

"How long was I connected?"

"Less than a minute," came the reply. "You put on the set, called for pen and paper, wrote something, then pulled off the set."

Malthusan showed him the paper with the script. "Did you see this in there?"

"That, and a whole lot more," Mason answered. "We have a new problem."

* * *

"Andrael?" Jaelon said after Mason had gathered the others and briefed them. They were arrayed around Mason's front room, each one showing varied states of surprise at the revelation. "I am not familiar with the name."

They were seven now, the Knights and the cell together. Mason couldn't help but note that this made them the most powerful cell in North America and wondered if the same had occurred to Azrael and was known to the mysterious Andrael.

"A recruit, perhaps?" Overguard ventured.

The Knights turned somber faces to him.

"Unthinkable," Populus said. "Such a betrayal shall never happen."

Overguard stared dubiously at them and looked at Mason, who shrugged.

"Reinforcement, perhaps?" Meeker postulated.

"More likely," Martin said. "Although why the name has never appeared before is a mystery."

"Not every rebel was identified to Man," Malthusan said. "Ours is not the only world under His command, you know."

"Enough," Jaelon snapped. Malthusan grimaced at her but fell silent. "What is important is the information about Azrael's organization," Jaelon went on. "This is what we need to hit him in such a way he can be eliminated with a minimum of collateral damage."

"Collateral damage?" Overguard asked.

"Minions like Azrael do not vacate easily," Malthusan answered. "I believe you remember a certain Teutonic despot of the middle 20th century? Azrael's rank and standing is equal to that one's."

Overguard snorted. "You're pulling my leg."

Malthusan frowned at him. "Did you truly believe that one was not a Minion?"

Overguard started to answer, then shrugged helplessly. "I suppose not."

"If we are to take on Azrael, we must strike from inside, just as this Andrael appeared to intend," Jaelon said.

"So, what's the plan, then?" Tripp spoke up.

"We cannot afford to confront him directly," Jaelon said. "The price in lives would be too high." She shook her head and looked at Martin. "How long would it take to fix one of those sets for each of us?"

Martin looked from her to the I/O and thought for a moment. "Not long. A few hours at most."

She nodded. "Then it is time The Army learned how to fight in another medium."

EPILOGUE

"Jenkins is dead," the message said.

Andrew Nicholson tapped the delete key with his immaculately manicured middle finger. The computer email account dutifully consigned those words to oblivion. He leaned back and surveyed his opulently decorated office. Art from the farthest reaches of Catalina Industries' empire adorned it. Furniture of the finest and richest woods graced its space. The computer itself was embedded within his desk, a state of the art heads up interface displaying its holographic controls on a diaphanous screen suspended by nearly invisible nanofilaments.

"The satellite security footage you requested is now available," the computer AI chimed.

"Show me," he commanded, steepling his long fingers before him and leaning his head back into the luxurious chair specifically designed to hug the contours of his lean frame.

The picture was artificially enhanced to correct for the

darkness and distance, but he had no trouble following the final few moments of Jenkins' life. The blanking of the screen at the end, when Jenkins cried out that last time, puzzled him. What could have blinded the satellite just there? Not that it really mattered that much. It was probably just a technical glitch, an errant cloud, or a bit of space debris obscuring the view. The technicians would figure it out and have it fixed if necessary.

It annoyed him that Jenkins had fouled up his assignment. What had gone wrong? All the man had to do was get some files from the Panama branch. And who were these people? How had they become involved with Jenkins?

"Identification on the other subjects," he instructed.

One by one, the faces of a woman and two men appeared in the display with the caption "Unknown. No records." Nicholson raised an eyebrow at that. Catalina was privy to the intelligence files of nearly every nation on Earth. It was incomprehensible there should be nothing on these people anywhere.

The next two faces did have records, but their names meant nothing to him. Jonah Mason? John Tripp? The information accompanying them gave no clue as to why they might be in contact with Jenkins, much less why they would kill him.

He frowned. He didn't like mysteries, especially when they interfered with an ongoing operation. He stabbed a finger at the intercom.

"Get in here," he snapped, then cut the connection with another annoyed jab.

Two men in dark uniform suits entered and stood respectfully silent as Nicholson rose from his desk and turned to look out the window wall at the city landscape. The United States Capitol building glowed amber in the fading sunlight just a few blocks away.

"Find them," he said without turning. "Find them and bring them to me."

The men glanced at the two faces in the computer display, then left without a word.

ABOUT THE AUTHOR

H. David Blalock has been a writer of speculative fiction for over 35 years. His work, heavily influenced by the science fiction and horror writers of the early twentieth century, has appeared in anthologies, magazines, webzines, and novels. Educated in the US and the Panama Canal Zone, he currently lives in the Memphis, Tennessee area.

For more information about David and his work,
check his website at
ThranKeep.com

Check out the following pages to see more from

All Seventh Star Press titles available in print and an array of
specially priced eBook formats.

Visit www.seventhstarpress.com for further information.

Connect with Seventh Star Press at:
www.seventhstarpress.com
seventhstarpress.blogspot.com
www.facebook.com/seventhstarpress

Epic Urban Fantasy-The Rising Dawn Saga

A shadow falls across the world, and realms beyond, as a war that has raged since the dawn of time itself draws closer to a decisive clash. As groups aligned with a movement called The Convergence speed up their efforts to bring about a global economic and legal order, resistance mounts after the host of a syndicated radio show, Benedict Darwin, discovers the true nature of a virtual reality device that has come into his possession. The Rising Dawn Saga will take you into mythical, supernatural realms as it unfolds, as the most unlikely of individuals rise to confront powers that have existed since before the world began.

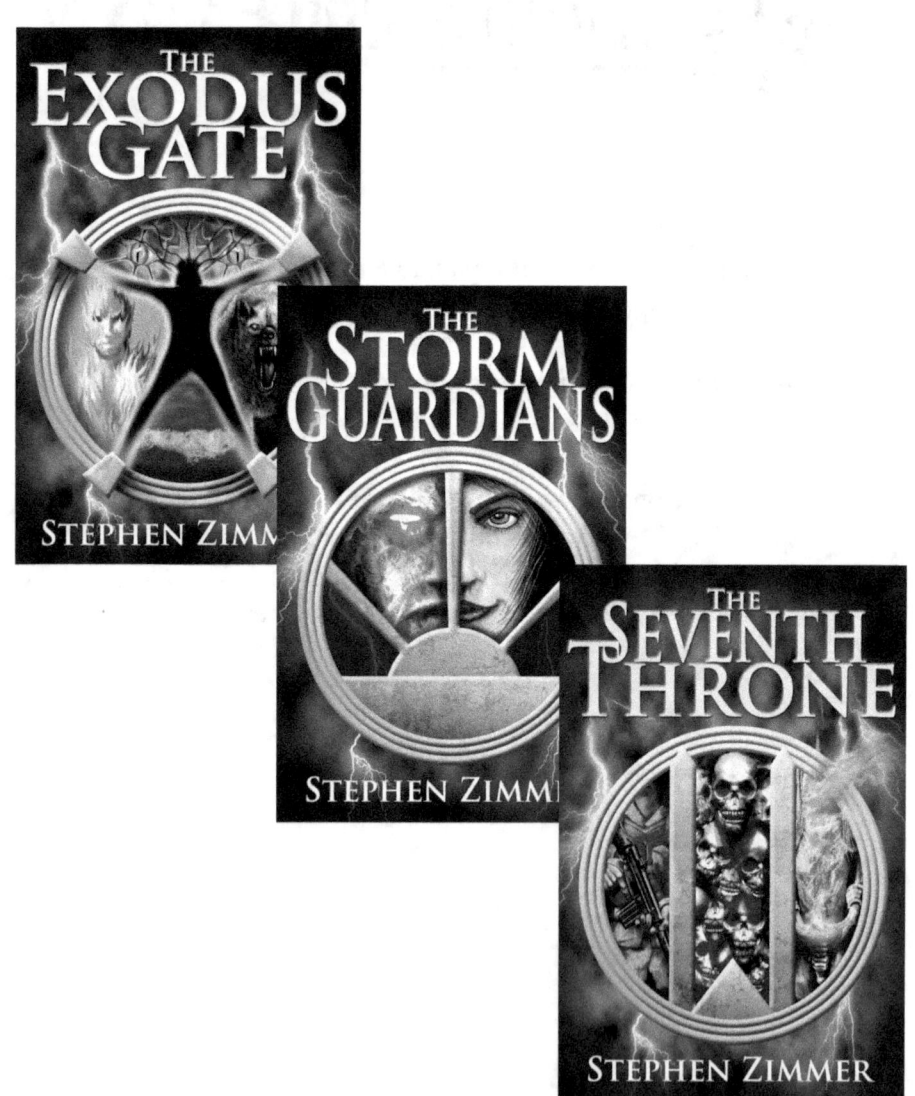

Book One: The Exodus Gate

"With The Exodus Gate author Stephen Zimmer sets the stage for an adventurous new science fiction fantasy series that is sure to entertain the reader from beginning to end. Zimmer has weaved a tale of fantastic realms populated with exotic creatures. Keep a sharp eye out for this new series."
-Mark Randell, Yellow30 Sci-Fi

"…a book that Fantasy Book Review recommends for lovers of thoughtful-fantasy. It is also a book with an ending that is near-prophetic, written as it was before the world's economic meltdown."
-Fantasy Book Review

Book Two: The Storm Guardians
ISBN: 978-0982565636

"This novel transports me from my bedroom to the edge of an upcoming storm — a battle to be fought by incredible villains and noble heroes of all forms. I love Zimmer's imagination, as each of his creatures play a pivotal role in the bigger picture. Unfortunately, for every auspicious being there is an ominous beast lurking in the shadows. Zimmer's weave of fantasy and religious fables leaves the reader sated"
-Bitten By Books

"The scope of The Storm Guardians is massive, opening up and expanding on the conflict only hinted at in The Exodus Gate. The intrigue and action promised in the first book is fully developed and mercilessly exhibited. The Storm Guardians is a non-stop thriller that lives up to the promise of The Exodus Gate and points at an even more amazing denouement in the final book of the series. Once again, Zimmer has used his command of cinematic imagery to give us a spectacular vision of war both heavenly and hellish. Two thumbs up on this one."
-Pure Reason Book Review

Book Three: The Seventh Throne
ISBN: 978-0983740247

NOW AVAILABLE!

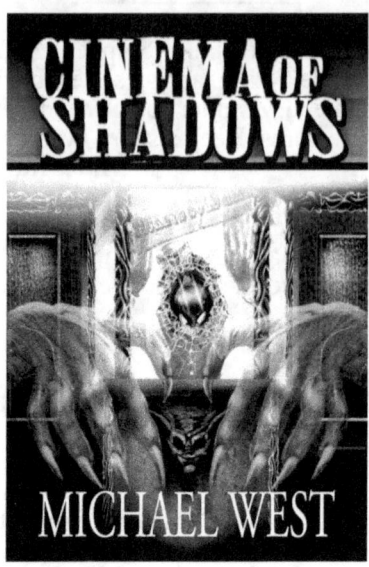

Trade Paperback ISBN: 9780983740209
eBook ISBN: 9780983740216

Welcome to the Woodfield Movie Palace.

The night the Titanic sank, it opened for business...
and its builder died in his chair.   In the 1950s, there was
a fire; a balcony full of people burned to death. And years
later, when it became the scene of one of Harmony, Indiana's
most notorious murders, it closed for good.   Abandoned,
sealed, locked up tight...until now.

Tonight,   Professor   Geoffrey   Burke   and   his
Parapsychology students have come to the Woodfield in
search of evidence, hoping to find irrefutable proof of a
haunting. Instead, they will discover that, in this theater,
the terrors are not confined to the screen.

Now Available from Seventh Star Press, Steven Shrewsbury's hard-hitting, heroic fantasy novel THRALL, featuring illustrations and cover art by fantasy artist Matthew Perry!

Trade Paperback ISBN: 9780983108634
eBook ISBN: 9780983108641

For Gorias La Gaul...
Deliverance Will Come

Set in the mists of ancient times, *Thrall* tells the story of Gorias La Gaul, an aging warrior who has lived for centuries battling the monstrosities of legend and lore. It is an age when the Nephilum walk the earth, demonic forces hunger to be unleashed, and dragons still soar through the skies ... living and undead. On a journey to find one of his own blood, a young man who is caught in the shadow of necromancy, Gorias' path crosses with familiar enemies, some of whom not even death can hold bound.

Thrall is gritty, dark-edged heroic fantasy in the vein of Robert E. Howard and David Gemmell. It is a maelstrom of hard-hitting action and unpredictable imagery, taking place within an incredible antediluvian world. In Gorias La Gaul, *Thrall* introduces an iconic new character to the realms of fantasy literature. Thrall invites the reader to go on a perilous journey where it is not a matter of whether one has the courage to die, but whether one has the courage to live.

All Seventh Star Press titles available in print and an array of specially priced eBook formats. Visit www.seventhstarpress.com for further information.